A Volunteer's Chronicle

and Collected Experiments

Dean C. Gardner

PublishAmerica
Baltimore

Hardcover 9781456005726
Softcover 9781456005733
eBook 9781627098489
PUBLISHED BY PUBLISHAMERICA, LLLP
www.publishamerica.com
Baltimore

Printed in the United States of America

Dedicated to the memory of the now:
the Age of Babel.

TABLE OF CONTENTS

CHAPTER 1: ON THE WAY

True or false:

The possible is to imagination

As faith is to the actual?

So
He was the prototype
Of the seeker of Truth
The model of an archetype.

So
It was for him
To grasp the invisible
The spaces between the lines
As time and times and a half
Drifted
Through the integrated collective
To grasp being there.

So
He found his life
Thrown into the war
Of principalities.

He left as the son of a chief
To before the Big Bang
Returning as Chaplain to his tribe.

His father taught him long ago:

To always look
A gift horse in the mouth,
Because trouble is always free;

That blood is not a pretty color
On concrete anywhere,
While sunshine is always a pretty color
everywhere;

It does not take
An eternity for a man
To bleed to death,
But for some, even eternity
Is too short to be redeemed.

Thus
His father taught him
To dine on manna first thing
As a start every morning
Since life was not
For the faithless.

It was not
That he had many loves
In his life
But he had his share
Of true loves here and there
Always one at a time
Because that is the way
He learned it from the chief
His father.

He lived
To always be true to a true spirit.

Some fell along the way
But when one did
It never was by his choosing
But by the calling
From beyond any here and now;

It simply is what it was.

He was ordained
Chaplain Eagle Hawk
A child of The Word
From north of Dixie
Not a carpet bagger
Not a Benedict Arnold
But a relocated patriot
As an expatriated volunteer.

He was
Sent from the other side
Of being and time
To the Valley of Olympus
In Tennessee
And he was versed in the byways
Of Red Skin lore
As a North American mutt
That went somewhere
Always at once.

But then,
There was a puppet master
The king head
Of an apostate tribe
A Richard III
That consumed life.

As the puppet master
Of the Tweedledums
And one of the vilest demons
A powerfully lethal enigma
He led the attack
On the home of the brave
As the world
Looked on with no clue
Of the future
For a land from sea
To shining sea.

Demons directed
The children of infamy
To be bomb toting assassins
With the minds of nothing to lose
Because they were bred
On doublespeak.

What are the odds
Of getting out
Of life alive?

What are the odds
Of getting through
The day
With a little hope from friends?

Each day was a gauntlet.

When Chaplain Hawk came
Into a place
No one took notice
But whenever he left
The unregenerate felt emptiness
Suddenly
And all were curious
If his was the emblem of Truth
Or the badge of the beast
Because they could not
Understand his mask
As a seeker of Truth.

So
It is that all cling to hope
Never truly knowing clearly
Always seeking, always hoping
For blessed assurance.

It was not
That he took
More than he brought
But that he gave
What they could not grasp.

So
Some were predestined
To descend forever
Where there is no hope
Forever devoured
By hideous nightmares
Carved into their eternity
As the dice were cast
During the Crusade of the age
While others drifted off
In their wondrous dreams
Onto forevermore.

Predestination is not
A factor in linear time
But the will
Of The Unknown God
From a vertical column
Of time.

Destiny is
What one lives
Through linear time.

The head king's snarl
Creased minds
With an indelible terror.

To the question
Tweedledums were afraid to ask
Demons brought the answer
And some accepted
What was there
As truth.

For some
The Truth was always
Good News.

Hope is in some ways
A great gift from The Word
But even for Tweedledees
Even hope can be taken away
With the grafting in and cutting out
Of the members.

So
It is with fear and trembling
That one lives destiny.

For some
The Truth left them
Naked in their despair
Outliving themselves.

Eagle Hawk's eyes
Were not shifty
But steady
Not piercing but truly sensing
And with one look
He saw all that was there
As well as all
That was concealed
By seeing through the window
Of the integrated collective
Weighing connectivity
Against juxtaposition
Sensing the drift between the two
Reading the ground
Of what was meant to be
At any given time, at any given place.

All he wanted was to make it
Through the daily gauntlet
Being thankful for home
At the end of a long, long battle.

Eagle Hawk had been taught
How to be true
And for that teaching
He was thankful, as The Word
Moved him ever nearer
To the battle's edge
But hungry went
The head king
Powered by the corrupt
As the Tweedledums
Man, woman
And child became
devouring weapons
With maggots crawling
in their minds.

It was not
That Eagle Hawk was
For some and against others
Or against some
And for others;
It was that Chaplain Hawk
Was a seeker of Truth
And he was
There to pronounce
The substance
Of the matter that matters most
Within the reaches
Of being there.

The boundaries of sides
The issues pitting
One against the other
Seemed to him
Artificial constructs
Of thoughtless imaginings.

It was the very matter
Of the power of darkness
Against the Power of Light
And the way of Truth in life.

He knew how some
Saw themselves
As the center of it all
With inviolate opinions
Thrust upon the scene
And these carefully dwelt
Among all territories
With a hunger for power
As their source
As fallen stars, as agents
spoiled in rot.

Eagle Hawk was not
Of that breed.

His was not an opinion
A point of arbitration
An arrogant assertion
Or a thoughtless contention.

His was a being there
In the depth
Of what he was
Seeking a point to a direction
Where Truth found home.

Truth was never an opinion
And never an assault
But rather a revealing
With gentleness and mercy
As the Crusade grew long
Into a purer shade of purpose
As a strong sense of survival

Anchored the elements
Of time and being
Triggered and cued
As The Word so willed.

The power of Truth
Was not in the voice
Behind it
But the power
Intrinsic
To The Unknown God
With the sword of The Word
Thrust
Into the belly of evil;
Thus it was
A time to return
To what matters most
As the volunteers advanced
From the now.

Yes
There was such a thing
As Truth for Eagle Hawk
And it purposed his being
Into that which is there as long
As he kept with The Word.

In all that he was
With all he ever did
Chaplain Hawk had
An accomplice, a female figure
Giving him wonders of bliss
After she covered his feet.

Her name
Was Captain Anna Meta Lee
And she was the keeper
Of his might, the cloth

Of his being there
And his Southern half
Reportedly as a direct descendent
Of Robert E., himself.

Captain Anna Meta was not
Defined by the confines
Of Chaplain Hawk 's comings and goings
But by the Celestial Clocks
Gathered from her look
And placed in a book of swirling orbs
That shot through his workings
And sowings as prods
Toward Truth.

Hers was never a deception
But an honest reading
Of a concept from its inception
The speaking in the language
Of angels.

Chaplain Hawk learned
From her ways
That manipulation
Was the work of demons
While intervention was the work
Of The Word.

Captain Lee was close
To the center
Of what everything is about
And what was meant to be
As she configured the geometry
Of time and space
For all that she touched
With her slender fingers
With a wave of her delicate hands.

There was a mystery
To her talk
A ministry to her walk
As she spun a thread
Into the everlasting
As she wove a fabric
Of wine and bread.

Lee spoke
To the tree in the forest
And the forest of trees
To the possibility of mountains
And the mountains of possibility
So
She became Eagle Hawk's window
For endless, wondrous visions
In this life.

It was
That all that is
Met in the fierce fire
Of a night filled with thunder
Bringing a war call
Onto the dying end.

Captain Anna Meta Lee
Traced the image
Behind the thought
Of what was the seen
And what was the unseen
As she parted the veils
As she raised the shrouds
As she cleared the clouds
From the Truth, opening the eye
Of the integrated collective
While she inspected the within
And the projected out.

Lee lived
In the wilds of the unknown
And she found in Chaplain Hawk
A ride
That stretched
Through all that could be
And much of what could never be.

Chaplain Hawk embraced
This woman
For all that she was
The face behind and within
His being there
And Lee accepted
His forthright giving
As a testament of his life
Of his living breath
That caressed her heart.

They met
In a garden of tables and chairs
A day and a night
Of chairs giving rise
To a remnant
Of the free wind
With freedom's crackling fire,
The tables
Flowing with a glow of words
In drifts and layers of drifts
As meanings
As the rockers rolled by
As a window hung in the sky.

They met
Before the tick of any clock
Started time running out
Before the sun ever rose
And certainly before it ever set.

Their lives
Were the dominoes of eternity
Put in motion
As the little Truths of being
Form and substance;
Yet, they were
Of muscle, bone and blood
Of a vast pool of understanding
Of monuments of hope
As the moons of forever
Pointed toward their destiny
Because they knew The Word.

He
Was her faithfulness
And she
Was his dream
They becoming a hymn
From the heart of forevermore.

They were by design
With The Word
Beyond condemnation
And living by faith alone.

Upon their horizon
Joy rang true.

But then
In one moment
Demons fractured time
For all of time
As the Tweedledees' free will
Struggled against a curse.

The dominoes
Were hopelessly scattered
In pieces of debris
But in this garden
Of tables and chairs
A spirit rose
That would free believers
From darkness.

He would be known
As a Trumpet
of The Unknown God.

So
He wanted to be where
Time bled into space
For a while, to serve
To experience
The long race at a steady pace
To the stand
Where The Word kissed
His being with the beyond.

In a somewhere
Chaplain Hawk gathered
Men and women
Being the chosen children
And the remnant, hoping
To open their eyes to The Word
Before the end.

Is it written
That the mind is mightier
Than the heart?

So
One thinks through the mind
Feels through the heart
And understands
Through being there.

Chaplain Hawk longed
To leave behind
The confines of his own thoughts
And his own thinking
For a ride
Across a large divide
In the earth of being there
Because he heeded the call
Of Truth
To experience the raw nakedness
Of substance and form
And there he hoped to find
The handle of Truth
Gripped in part with understanding
That discerned art from rancor
The treasure buried under the filth
Of the self-righteous and others.

He longed for the sense
Of something beyond thingness
As the pursuit of Truth and beauty
Rumbled, an immense propounding,
The immersion
Of self beyond all dimensions.

So
The prayerful trance
Was a lesson learned.

To leave
The comforts of easy living
To cleave
Meaning out of a sense
Onto being
As the road led
Like a dangling thread
Through time, through space:
It could only have brought him
To a discerning point
Where turning to The Word
Could only come through an anointing
Of bread and wine.

He ever so hungered
For tours
Into the integrated collective
Ever so sought the horizons
Where all battles
Were yet to be fought.

It was
A season for probing.

Captain Anna Meta Lee
And Chaplain Hawk
Exchanged vows
In a quiet castle
On February 29th
In Ireland
She tucking the seven of hearts
In his coat
And he tucking her hands
In his pockets
And theirs was true love
For the while
As their first born
Sunday grew strong.

It is always already true:
Puppet masters play games
With power
But The Word plays
No games.

It was day by day
That Chaplain Hawk
And Captain Anna Meta
Gathered the way
Of true love
Riding the line
With fear and trembling
With joy and a cheerful heart.

It was time to head out
To hit the wind, to haul a load.

With Captain Anna Meta Lee
Wrapped around his body
Fitting his form like a fist
Chaplain Hawk pulled the throttle back
And they were rolling
To a holy war.

As they departed
From familiarity
As echoes of the known
Slipped away
In the rear view mirror
Their appetite for battle fattened
As they were donned in the full armor
Of The Unknown God.

Their thunder
Ripped through the rush
Of the road
Giving notice to all demons

That Captain Anna Meta Lee
And her man
Were on their way
For certain business.

Fear for them
Was contestable, being respectful
Of the ways and means of all life
But being afraid
Of nothing in the now
As long as they were
With The Word.

The road wound
Through hills and mountains
Through valleys and ravines
Across all of this side
Of what was known
Onto the dimensions
Of the unknown.

Then
The road
That led behind mind
Opened an eye with wings
To visions, soaring
Into the invisible
After a troupe of the remnant
Had been gathered.

Pulling their rolling
Thunder and steel
To the side
of the straight and narrow
They stood down only
to hear a peel
A sound out of nowhere
separating
the quick from their marrow.

It was
A sound of debilitating pain
A shrill squeal
Of un-grounding torment
A confession of being there
A procession into terror
And they stepped back
As a chill crept down their spine
Upon hearing this searing whine.

It was by the gift
Given to Chaplain Hawk
That he learned that Tweedledums
Are forever banned
From having freedom
And are destined to leach life
From the breath of humankind
Because there is always already
That which is good and right
And there is that which is
An abomination, siding with evil;
Yet,
Demons thought
They could gain a life
By dissolving their prey
Into the blood of fear.

The time became
A dawn of a day to be
To see with a clearer vision
To cut away the wounds
of form without substance
With a clean incision
To periscope through the division
Of time and space
To reface the masks
Of intrepid derision
As a chill crept down the spine
Of Eagle Hawk and Anna Meta
Upon hearing this searing whine.

The sky lit up
With a sliver of silver
An eastern cry of light
From the cistern of the night
As their ride through the darkness
Had undressed the deep
As their stopping
before the steep of day
Unseated the hell of what was there
As a chill crept down their spine
Upon hearing this searing whine.

Reaching into the heart
Of a day to be
Revealing the nakedness
Of what the mind would see
They touched the stone
The muscle, the bone of dawn
As light rose upon the scene
As meaning gathered
From what they lived
As a chill crept in their heart
Upon hearing this searing whine.

The dawn woke up to the cry
Of Truth.

Up from the North
Swarmed a cloud of sparrows
At first appearing
As a shadow filling the sky
That advanced upon the setting
Where Captain Anna Meta
Filled Chaplain Hawk
With the might of faith
At the side of the road
As they stood wearing the wind.

As a swirling mass
Of molten flesh
Approached their horizon
Chaplain Hawk looked into Lee's eyes
Hoping for her to trigger
Some form of message
A rhyme to the scene, but all she did
Was inhale a deep breath
With her eyes closing
As the swarm of sparrows
Gathered around their feet.

So
That which appeared
As an attack
Was a ghost of possibility.

The sparrows covered the ground
And they pecked at the earth
Feeding on the substance
That was there for them
As their chatter filled
The air
With an advancing passage of time
Into the integrated collective.

Captain Anna Meta Lee
Saw the common sparrow
As being always busy
With never a moment
For repose
Twitching, flitting
Pecking at the earth
Always busy
Always immersed in activity.

Their sound
Arose from beyond the common place
Not laced with special knowledge
But a sound
That wears the face
Of what matters most.

Their wisdom
Was in the common place
With being immersed in The Word.

Chaplain Hawk watched them
With thoughtfulness
As he looked after them
Always allowed, always allowing.

As quickly
As the swarm
Of sparrows came
They dispersed
Leaving no trace
On the landscape
Of the here and now
But only fading impressions
In memory
But welcomed always.

It was as if
The ordinary was there
As Chaplain Hawk
And Captain Anna Meta Lee
Triangulated who they were
As she then penetrated
The quick of his time and space
To unleash their presence
Into another dimension.

They took
A four dimensional reality
And removed depth
So
All and everything
Was on a flat plane
For the conscious.

Then, they aligned
The crosshairs on the target
That point being
Toward entrance for the needle
Of their eye.

Piercing times and a half
From a parabola of time
They flung themselves
Through a target
Only to return the other dimensions
Into the form
Of what had been imaged
From anchor, to trigger, to cue
And back
From alpha to omega
Through a delta, and back
Through being there
Onto time and space
As witness to The Word.

Thus, began
The while
Of altered reality
A physics defined
By a revealed threshold
Where they would pioneer
Around and about.

Yes, that is how it all began
As the prayerful trance
Superseded time and space.

"En garde. Tres bien." Was
Said through the integrated collective
As Eagle Hawk met
His dream garden in only
A true Captain Anna Meta.

"Yes, gather the Tweedledees
Together," went the oracle
"even those abducted."

So
Chaplain Hawk turned his back
Away from obsidian stone
And his love
Captain Anna Meta Lee
Drank their powerful roan
Because a remnant of Tweedledees
Would live on forever inducted."

Then Eagle Hawk sat down
Before a demon
The source of the shrill cry
To face the meaning
Of what was there
As he pulled himself
Onto the ground before myth
With solitary focus
Through the will
Of The Unknown God.

That was the way
It was in the valley of Olympus
Where freedom of being
Was a wondrous treasure

As a demon landed an assault
Straight from hell.

So
Eagle Hawk entered
A prayerful trance
As all and everything
Entered the metaphor
Of being and time.

"Chaplain Hawk ," the demon said,
"how is your wand?"
And then it cackled.

Coming through time and space
An explosion erupted.

A vendetta was signed,
Sealed and smoked
The clever demon outwitted
By its foolish joke
As Eagle Hawk's faith held true
Before the demon's incantation
Spoke
His end before time.

There was no
lucky number for demons
For invading Chaplain Hawk
Because his prayerful trance
Dissolved them away
While he headed
Down the road
To meet with the rest
Of the rolling thunder.

Captain Lee
Looked to Chaplain Hawk
For an explanation
As she stirred
In her times and a half.

"Tres bien," said another demon
"tres bien. Tres bien."

The wind blew
Across a river of ways
As tomorrows rustled
Into days and times of days
As moons rubbed
Being always already there
Again and again.

This puppet master,
A wickedly wicked thing
Captain Anna Meta fought
In the bowels of being,
As the wind and fire of eternity
Begat an army onto forevermore,
A race of principalities
As the prayerful trance
Was the right medicine
for celestial wounds.

Captain Anna Meta raised
Her thumb to image
what was there
The model, Chaplain Hawk 's first
Born daughter
As the mix of gentle airs
Filled with spirits of water
When she leaned one dimension
Into another with care.

It was the first touch of spring
Lovely, beauteous, peaceful
That they longed for
As fear crept through bones
Of the living dead;
Yet
The tide comes in
The tide goes out
And demons interfere
With the gravity of being there.

"En garde." said Captain
Anna Meta for good
As obsidian is to stone
As ebony is to wood
As darkness knows no light.

Across countless dimensions
The Tweedledees sped
Upon their own thunder machines
Capturing a place beyond
The myths of the dead
Where oblivion anchored doom.

So
The remnant was ready
To fight the good fight.

It was a call to arms
That triggered the remnant
A drawing of energies
Based upon their belief
That no demon could move.

Captain Lee set a steady course
Through times and a half
So
It became the Tweedledees

Led by The Word
And followed by Eagle Hawk
As their faith brought
The Tweedledums down
To a pit in hell
Until conjured thoughts crumbled
Before the way of Truth in life.

And then, with a wave
Across the nations
The paranormal opened
Illusion
As new sensations
And some followed it
To their demise.

So
The keepers
Of time held time
As metaphor
Through the prayerful trance
Where hours were days
And days were half times
With Eagle Hawk
And his lovely
Watching the celestial clock
Carry the demons
Across a sky of pines
To a hell
Beyond a parabola of time.

It was at this confinement
Through metaphor
That thought begat
Memories shedding the grip
Of the past
As space placed time
In a two dimensional reality.

Night was ever so dark
In the darkness of the mind
As seeing more out of what
Was there moved reason
Into the tracing of thoughts anchored
By metaphor.

As being groaned
For mercy
The Word blessed
The faithful.

Then
Tweedledums set
The anchors for mayhem
To raise the advance
Of guilt and shame again and again
The Accuser's trigger
In the heart of mankind.

CHAPTER 2: THE OVERFLOWING

True or false:

The mind is to the unknown

As The Word is to being there?

So
It was for Chaplain Hawk
To understand the substance
Of being and time.

So
It was a war fought
In the heart and mind.

Beyond what was there
In thought, word and deed
Chaplain Hawk
Knew the hurt of pain
Enduring a devastation
Beyond personal annihilation
As a hellfire Mariah blew
Across his mind
But with The Word
He learned to find
The hope
That made true
The passage onto forevermore
With a greater power
Than an incanted elixir
Of time with space
A glorious wealth
Of a precious space
Where Truth purposed beauty
In magnificent iterations
Grand in a cut across being there.

His father showed him
That for every hat
There was a rabbit.

It was that long, long ago
In a universe
More vintage

Than the here and now
A parabola of time
Surfaced
And turned the corner
Of what was there
In Truth.

It was all
A matter of imaging
In the conscious
Throwing that image back
Along the way
From conscious to preconscious
To subconscious and unconscious;
Then reversing the sequence
Backing out carefully
Pulling up from the brainstem;
Thus, proceeded
A parabola of time
Through the prayerful trance.

Then he was pricked
By the song filled tongue
Of the land
Learning that children
Of The Unknown God
Were the promise
Made to The Word.

Inexplicable phenomena arouse
In the year of another dimension:
A fear for humankind
Because there was no way
For Tweedledees
To anticipate Tweedledums
Or to understand the reason
For demonic origin.

So
It would be war.

So
The demons
Were those who thought
They could steal the hopes
Of a man by writing on his tongue,
And they could set anchors, triggers
And cues to alter hopes
But Destiny's child had the last word
Since The Word birthed the right
Of a being to be.

It was
That being there
With The Word was hope itself
And that Chaplain Hawk's heart
Stirred with the light of hope
Upon knowing The Word.

He knew
That hope could not be found
Everywhere, at times nowhere
And within his geometry
He found the indwelling
Of a promise
In witnessing the Truth
While following the way
When he only knew
The ache in being there;
So
There were always spirits, demons
And puppet masters
While being there.

Spirits were among the principalities
And they all were good;

They were the promise chosen
To carry life in Truth.

Puppet masters were evil
And were all of the devil.

Demons were assassins
In time and space
And the soldiers
Of puppet masters.

It was autumn
Among the hills of Volunteers
The trees living through a celebration
Of color.

Colliding with the ramparts
Of the paranormal
Brought Chaplain Hawk onto a place
Where hope was past
But given the time
He endured;
For he learned long ago
When enervation persists
Life insists.

But it was war
With rampant pain
Capturing the mind.

Then
They mounted their motors
Growling through space and time.

He found
That in the paranormal
He was alone
Alone with demons of darkness

And the rage
That they rained down
In torrents of hellfire.

Although this time
Chaplain Hawk launched there
With Captain Anna Meta Lee
The paranormal divided
Being and time
A fearsome projection
That obliterated hope
Causing a deep trembling
That united the who of pain
To the what of the horrific.

So
Memories
Of war ripped him apart.

But then again
For a woman
As Captain Lee who wears
Her faith before a good fight
A man yearns
In his emptiness
Confessing to The Word
The certain Way, the indelible Truth
And the everlasting Life.

How love grows hope.

Captain Anna Meta Lee
Was The Unknown God's gift
To a man
And his tribe
As an immutable force
Voiding the hold
Of the puppet masters
Onto the nevermore.

Chaplain Hawk beheld
A land of promise
As the hope
That exceeds understanding
Was the blessing
For this era.

So
Where does
Admiration end
And idolatry begin?

So
Where then
Is covetousness?

So
It is said
That I am The Word
Thou shall have no idols
Before me.

So
It would be war again
As the heart pounded in turmoil.

Rumbling down the road
Chaplain Hawk seized
Being there
Guided by The Word.

The pleasant fragrance
Of the rising mist
The hills having found their bliss
Launched beauty in the wonder
Of a day to be

So
One took it day by day
As cards were given
From the top of the deck.

How trivial
Was pain of the here
And now
While facing the promise
Of forevermore.

So
Chaplain Hawk always
Remembered
That the cold of winter
Was fleeting
In the eye of forevermore
That the pain
Of today would become
A myth buried in the past.

So
The Tweedledees
Were granted
An age of hope
Where despair would not
Touch them.

It was
The pervading wind
From the deep South
That brought rain
For a day
A solid reign of The Word
And a spirit was driven
Into the hearts
Of the remnant
That spoke a beauty

Of promise into a country
Of mountains and forests.

It was
The promise of being
Alongside the rise
Of a sun
A morning of wonder
Bound to eternity
And woven into rock
With the breath of courage.

The wind fortified
The stand
Of the Tweedledees
Against the tyranny
Of puppet masters
And the delusions
Of the Tweedledums.

They had become
The plague
Engineered upon humanity.

And so it was written
As long as there was
The Word with them,
The Tweedledees
Would be the strength on earth
A remnant sealed with The Word.

As the demons
Of what was there
Struck a deep numbness
Across the horizon
Of a being's timber
Colored with an autumn profusion,
Chaplain Hawk eased his mind

Onto a another view
Cool and friendly.

He saw
Captain Anna Meta Lee tending
To what was there
Her smile carrying across the way
As gallant men gathered
The souls of the living
And the dead.

There was no longer
A tomorrow
For so many
Who had manipulated
Being there
With compass and ruler
With reason and intelligence
Because they were without
The substance that mattered
In the long run of destiny.

Where intellect failed
Faith prevailed.

Where logic went silent
Faith spoke in abundance.

Time evaporated
Beneath an autumn heat.

Space dissolved
Into the blue sky.

The river weighed the properties
Of despair.

Silence
Mended a day
Of tribulation.

Shadows
Consumed themselves
In a rip of terror.

From the threads
Of light
Swaying through the clouds
Captain Anna Meta Lee launched
An armada of dreams
To delight
The chasms in twilight
As earth spun with purpose
Its body filled
With potent prayers.

There was
Among drifts of leaves
Gathering at the sides
Of the lane
A rise of light
Twinkling in the always
That love knew well.

It was the love for The Word
That glued Chaplain Hawk
To Captain Anna Meta Lee
A bond of the living
Onto the living
As the sun shone
Through the branches
As the clouds fed harmony
To a hungry earth
And Captain Anna Meta Lee
Served an encouraging word

With a hand free in the air
Stirring a horizon of liberty
And a faithfulness to being there.

Somethingness could be
The same as life
While nothingness always led
To a corruption of being and time.

Dusk
Birthed life
To the living.

So
It was war that was
Meant to be
As agony rocked the mind.

One king
And two jacks
Set the range of fair
As a blind spot erased time
From the eyes
That saw onto forevermore.

A pair, heart and diamond
Bled to the Tweedledums.

The deal was set.

Bids were made.

Two spades
Went to the king and jacks
While three queens
Went to the bullets.

So
The Tweedledums
Took
With a full house.

It was
A game they played
As a dither of the mind
Where things were settled
By the luck of the draw
And Chaplain Hawk sat
Heavy in his set
With planets swirling
Behind his eyes
With stars lighting the way
From beginning to end
Where eternity lifted an horizon
To where time configured space
Into a rhapsody of fragrances
Rich in their powers of healing.

So
The war had begun.

The road heard the thunder
Of their motors
Leading the way to Truth.

As the game ended
The Tweedledums
Turned nothingness inside out
Bleeding the face
Of substance into a thinning air
Bringing one to outlive oneself.

It was a war that devoured life.

It was a battle that stole hope.

Silence
Awoke dusk
Into darkness.

Amid the indigo
Known to the night
Dark blood roared
In the vastness
Of the pitch
As the moon
Cried out in a crimson hue
As a thought of meaning
Found a harvest tone
As stars emptied their light
Into the spine of a mind
Longing for the rise of a new day.

So
It was said
That all was meaningless
meaningless.

And then it was dawn
And the flight of raven hair
Pronounced the unknown
Alongside the known
In the hopeful groaning
That caught the rise
Of the sun's glory.

The air
Crisp and fresh
Awakened to the blood and bone
Of another day
A day told to the heart
Of what matters most.

The sparrows
Spoke of Truth
As if it was
A common language
Between the light and the wind
And Captain Anna Meta Lee
Gathered the way
Set by the rising sun.

So
manipulating the forces
Of celestial clocks,
The puppet masters altered
What was there
Selling it to the highest bidder:
The Tweedledums sold
Themselves out, taking the bid.

The way
Was thick with hope.

The way
Launched the moment
Into eternity.

The Tweedledees
Carried the dawn light
In their eyes.

The sparrows shared in the wonder.

From beyond The Big Bang
Chaplain Hawk learned
How naked was
The Truth in a dawn
Of wonder
How innocent
Wonder dawned
In the Truth.

Amid a rebirth, Chaplain Hawk
Waved the Tweedledees on.

Grabbing thunder by the throat
He hurled
The quick of lightning
Across the flawless sky
And the blue crashed in cries
As the Tweedledees
Built substance into mountains.

It was war.

It was
The ragged edge
Of a demon's thirst
For first blood
That brought hellfire
Onto the plain
As what was there
Screamed as Tweedledum's souls
Found the agony of their forevermore.

It was
The light of day
Clinging to bloodied meat
That taught the river
How to sing
Of liberty and justice
As the corpses of a day in battle
Soiled the earth with their lives.

As the Tweedledees
Rode the wind
Breathing fists of fire
The armies of clever wits
The Tweedledums
Withered into dust and ash

And Captain Anna Meta Lee served
A round of sweet hope
To the remnant.

Trembling
With the cries
Of the dead and the dying
The earth stuttered
In its orbit around the sun
And traveled to where
Time touched the mind.

Flesh
Begat pain.

Pain
Seized the breath
Of being.

Being gagged
On its own demise.

It was a rage of battle
Caught in the meat of being there.

There was
No escape from the boil of blood
Fueled by the demons.

The carnage
Of this brutal assault
Rose in the sky
As a mist of death
And the cock roaches
Grew fat on the carnage.

Dancing
Over the valleys of dried bones

The mountains erupted
With sounds of jubilation
As the Tweedledees axed
The witless wonders
The Tweedledums
And Captain Anna Meta Lee
deciphered
All of time with another
Stir of hope.

Destiny spoke a truth.

In the death of the witless
Was triumph
For the Tweedledees.

The battle waged
The victory won
The Tweedledees
Filled their hearts with song.

Reconfiguring time
The crows
Steadied the earth
In the sky.

As the sun
Headed toward the west
And the wind passed
For breathless
Captain Anna Meta Lee slipped
Into shades of silence
Rubbing the earth with her wild
And Chaplain Hawk eyed her
With hopefulness.

It was time for tenderness.

It had been
A day of battle
Of a fight fierce in blood
And now that the air thinned
To a quivering light
It was time for love
To restore the heart
With the heat of hope.

How she glowed
Through the coming dusk.

How she fueled the fire
Of Chaplain Hawk's hunger
As he looked
Upon the melody
Of her movements.

How heaving sighs
Fogged the skies
With passion.

As they touched, the twilight
Danced an epiphany.

Surrounding the darkness
Growing upon the earth
Captain Anna Meta Lee
Eclipsed the moon
With the eye
In the back of her mind
Moving shadows
And shades of shadows
To a hollow
Without dimensions
The heart of obsidian stone.

The air grew thick
With a violet hue.

She tossed the stars
Into a necklace that she wore
As her smile encompassed
The way of Truth.

There was
Understanding to the moment
A moment slick with passion.

There was only
The rub of the darkness
In the night.

Captain Anna Meta Lee
Sounded the jets
In the heart of Chaplain Hawk
Onto forevermore.

Growing thick with electricity
The air spun in widening gyres
As the apocalypse
Of being and time perfumed
Across the mountains
And the eyes of Tweedledees
Jubilant in their victory
Looked into the heavens
On wings of falcons
As the falconer voiced the cues
That triggered the anchors
Upon Chaplain Hawk's form.

There was
The purity of forever
Woven into the moment
A time that no longer hungered

For more;
Yet, more and more
Followed onto forevermore.

So
They were victorious.

Glowing in the night sky
The Tweedledees
Formed the dynasty
Of whole new constellations
As a pulse of life
Increased across the expanse.

It was in the night
That the sky
Swore allegiance
To the love
Of Chaplain Hawk
And Captain Anna Meta Lee
As the bond of two souls
Endured forevermore.

So
When the heavens
Smiled upon a soul
And the ground dreamt
Of decorating life across the land
As trees offered their limbs
To autumn hymns
As the grasses sang
Through the cool night
Clinging to the warmth
Of days of dreams
A man followed the way
Into the everlasting
Believing in the glory
That was The Word's.

There was only
The seeing between the lines
In the second look
At what could be.

So
When the mountains
Smiled at a soul
As the sun
Gathered a moment from the drift
Of being alongside a length of time
And the heart drank in
The soothing hope
That eased the mind
Into quiet breaths
A man set his feet
Onto forevermore.

As the tempest visits the door
And the windows quiver with fright
A woman asked a question
That had no answer.

So what is love?

A day and a night
Without light was only
A curious thought.

In the light
A mind gathers a look
Into the everlasting
The domain of the invisible.

So
When the sky
Lit with eternal bliss
Smiling onto a universe of time

Where a man entered
The heart of a woman
Where a woman remembered
The matter of what matters most
It was the moment
When Tweedledees lived
Onto eternity
With life abundant
For the everlasting
In good health, good spirits
As Chaplain Hawk launched
His dreams of splendor
With Captain Anna Meta Lee
Her aura, imprinted upon the fabric
Of his brainstem.

CHAPTER 3: AN EXCURSION

True or false:

Ideation is to the magically revealed

As Truth is to the mysteriously invisible?

By being allowed and allowing
It was good for Chaplain Hawk
To be there
Among groves of stars
That lit eternity
Upon a rock
That swallowed the void
Near a river of song
That revealed the secrets
Of mind filling mysteries
As The Unknown God
Opened splendiferous wings
Of fire and smoke.

Eagle Hawk seized
The farthest side of the universe
Pulling the treasures
Of unthinkable Truths
Into a center and down to earth
Where Captain Anna Meta Lee rested
Her hair blown by the breath
Of forever in the everlasting.

From its depths
The earth howled
A forlorn cry.

There was a stir
In the reaches of the forest
A type of nervous twitching
In the boughs and limbs
Of trees confounded
By the moment.

Curious as ever
The night sky looked on
Trembling in its glitter.

Dean C. Gardner

On the knoll
Where Captain Anna Meta Lee
Reclined
Half asleep, half awake
A great blue heron landed
Its eyes like burning phosphorous.

Mounted upon the heron rode
A figure
A gold dust wolf
Not a man pursuing
An impossible dream
But a being in time and space
Armed with a glowing lance
To skewer the demons
That haunted souls;
However, Captain Lee waved it off
Because her dream was a light
Of certain pleasure
Anchored with trigger set
And the cue called.

Looking at time
Chaplain Hawk smiled
A pirouette into the air.

The heron and darkness
Flew onto the moon.

Near a bush
Still full with leaves
In this late autumn night
Was a figure frozen
In a quiet stream of sensing
And spinning around it
Were swirling lights
A nucleus of being
Surrounded by electrons

Of what was there
Certain in uncertainty
As they broke away
From the spine
Of what was meant to be.

It was an image
That was anchored deep
Within the brainstem of the mind.

It was an image
Where what could never be
Took form.

It was an impression thrown
From the reaches of impossibility
Across an arc of the believable
And it was called
The integrated collective.

There was
The figure of a tree
With branches as tentacles
Swirling through fists of fire
That whirled a sound
Of eerie tones
A piercing undulation
From the subtext of darkness
As the fury of its gyrations
Flung globs of space through time
As the hands of clocks
Slowly liquefied into a wondrous brew:

Chaplain Hawk strained to discern
The source, the meaning
Of the image near that bush
As Captain Anna Meta Lee returned
To her light filled dream

That gave her folds of pleasure
As some Tweedledees gathered
Before this obtuse spectacle
Unnerved in their stand.

It was a mysterious image
Traced within their horizon
Of time.

In the trunk
Of this tree of tentacles grew
An eye conspicuous in its irregularity
Having two irises, two pupils
With one sucking in
Fists of fire
While the other gushed out
A flood of molten flesh
And within this eye
Were the workings of times and a half
A mechanism that expanded the moment
Into a parabola of time
Where the molten flesh took form
As Captain Anna Meta cooed
In her rest
Her dreams manifested
From the wilds of her heart.

It was that what the heart
Knew for sure
The mind could not divine
As an unearthed soul
Appeared in the close at hand.

Captain Anna Meta Lee
exercised the muscle
Of a mountain
As The Word took hold
In the fight against demons.

Chaplain Hawk started
Allowed and allowing some more
Through the deep connection
Toward this incredible thing
And the Tweedledees
Pulled him back
Although all he wanted
Was a closer look.

A mist, thick and spirited
Was settling across the scene.

The river leaped from its bed
Filling the night sky
With a crystalline chorus
Of the integrated collective.

What was the meaning
Of the interlude?

After the thought took form
After the molten mass solidified
It appeared as the face of The Word
Bloodied and in pain
At the point near departure
And He spoke with heavy breath,
"Forgive them Lord
For they know not what they do."

It is that what the heart
Knows for sure
The mind cannot divine;
Thus, thinking stops
Where sensing begins.

Chaplain Hawk tried and tried
To grasp what he saw:

The tree with tentacles
The eye with two irises, two pupils
The outpouring of flesh
The fists of fire
The agony of The Word
And His compassionate request;
But, the all of this time and a half
Defied understanding
As a leap into mystery.

All of what he saw
Seemed a process
That made no sense
To his mind
Yet, it happened;
It was there.

All the while
Captain Anna Meta Lee lay
Content in her rest
Oblivious to the vision.

What the heart sees
The mind cannot grasp.

Chaplain Hawk looked up
Searching the skies, the heavens
For some clue to this view
As sweat beaded on his forehead
As a fierce chill pierced his spine;
And feeling alone, no matter
How he strained his eyes
For focus and clarity
All his mind saw
Was a blur of darkness.

His heart knew tragedy
The tragedy of the scene

The tragedy of knowing
That he may never understand
This or any vision.

Closing his eyes
Chaplain Hawk covered his face
With his hands
And fell to his knees.

Of course,
The Tweedledees understood
What he was going through
Because they were as perplexed
As Chaplain Hawk, and they put
Their hands on him
As they bowed their heads.

When he opened his eyes
The vision was gone
As the wind
Orchestrated clouds
Around the moon.

Together
He and the Tweedledees
Built a fire at the river's edge
Determined to wait the night out
Searching the flames for reasons
That seemed nowhere.

They sat around the fire
Listening to the flames crackle
As they poked the embers
With sticks.

It was not only
The incongruity and disconnectedness
Of the experience

But the purpose
Of it happening at all
Not only what it meant
But why it should be.

The night grew still
As the wind quieted.

All that could be heard
Was the voice of the fire.

Captain Anna Meta Lee rested
With a smile beneath closed eyes.

As dawn began
To light the sky
They let the fire die
But even in the hope
Of a new day
They had no explanation
For the vision
They all had witnessed.

In stillness a question loomed:
Was humanity a principality?

It was that what was there
That mystery in the darkness
Became the no more and no less
Than the unfathomable.

Captain Anna Meta Lee stirred
And then stretched
As she slowly awakened
Bundled in a blanket and ground cloth.

Kneeling beside her
Chaplain Hawk swept

Through her long brown hair
From across her face
And placed his hand
Upon her cheek.

She kissed his finger tips.

Eagle Hawk started to tell her
What happened in the night
But she interrupted him
Because she wanted
To tell him of her dream, first.

"I dreamt I was right here
Asleep, alone with the river.

I heard the river
Its soothing flow
And felt a gentle nudge
At my feet.

It was soft and warm.

In my dream, I knew
That I did not know
What it was
Because I knew I was asleep.

This furry creature
Exuded gentleness
A deep kindness
That I knew I wanted
So
In the dream
I pretended to sleep
So
I would not frighten him away.

Just as I had hoped
He came to my side
And then curled
On my body.

He smelled rich
With a tender wildness.

For the longest time
I grew more and more intoxicated
With his penetrating
And exotic fragrance.

I can remember
Seeing the hills and mountains swaying
Surrounded with swirling lights
In a very dark sky.

When I opened my eyes
To see him in my dreams
I caught a glimpse
Just before he disappeared.

He was a wolf
A beautiful, long-haired silver wolf.

What a beautiful creature
He was
And so very loving."

Chaplain Hawk 's face grew puzzled.

He could not understand
Why she did not feel frightened.

A wolf has jaws and teeth;
A wolf can bite – he thought
And voiced his confusion.

"Oh honey," she replied
"don't you see?
This silver wolf was you."

Now
He was even more confused.

Then, she asked him
To tell her of the vision
But he shrugged his shoulders
Smiled
And said it was unimportant.

He did not want
To spoil her good mood.

She prodded him for the seeing
But he changed the subject
By saying it was time to leave
Time to get some breakfast.

All the Tweedledee band
Mounted their choppers
Their baggers, trikes and scooters
Heading out, riding down the road
That wound through the mountains
As the trees, barren, and fleshy conifers
Struck up toward the heavens.

Chaplain Hawk and Captain Lee
Were toward the middle of their pack
Not being the leaders
Not being the trailers
Simply one with the group.

Soaking up the mist
The sun rose with warmth.

As the road went up
With a deep drop to the right
With a sheer rise to the left
The road hewn out of a cliff
They slowed
Because the way was unknown
And the unknown leered treacherously.

Chaplain Hawk thought
Of the vision
He saw the night before
Such agony on the face of The Word
And yet with a penetrating plea
Asking The Unknown God
To forgive His persecutors.

Although he knew the words
From Scripture, they did not register
In his heart, until he realized
The physical torment upon His face
Juxtaposed by The Word's prayer
Asking for His oppressors
To be innocent of His agony.

The rest of the vision
The tree of tentacles, the fists of fire
The eye as it was
Were superfluous staging
That pointed to A Great Truth.

"God so loved the world
That He gave His only begotten Son
And for all who believe in Him
They shall have eternal life."

Boulder in the road.

Rocks scattered about.

A time and a half to stop.

Staying a short distance back
The tail runner
Stood by his black bagger
Holding a yellow flag
To warn oncoming traffic
Of the road hazard.

The rest of the Tweedledees
Gathered together
Discussing the situation
Examining the debris on the road.

Because they figured that it
Had fallen from the strata above
And not from the heavens
They agreed
To do what they could
To fix the situation.

One does not alter
Acts of The Unknown God;
One intercedes
With the acts of faith.

Some carried the rocks
To the side, while others
Fit their muscle
To move the boulder.

The bolder was large
Heavy, cumbersome
And it would not roll.

It took muscle.

It took sweat.

Slowly
It yielded to the muscle
Of the Tweedledees.

After a time
That drained them
Of what they were
That seemed to stretch
Beyond what could be
They dragged the boulder
To the side of the road
So
Traffic could pass
In safety.

It took them over a time
To move this boulder about ten feet
But they did it.

It was done.

Chaplain Hawk thought
Of the myth of Sisyphus
The man who each day
Would roll a large stone
Up a mountain
Only to have it roll down
The other side.

Each day
The same thing, rolling
The same, large stone
Up the same steep mountain
Only to have it roll
Down the other side

As the Greek gods looked on
Entertained at Sisyphus
Ridiculing his life of futility.

Yes
Chaplain Hawk discerned, certainly
Other boulders would fall
Upon this stretch of road
But at least this one was
Put to rest.

So
The gods
Saw Sisyphus' endeavor
As ludicrous futility.

So
The gods
May view the Tweedledees effort
As equal folly.

So
The gods
Are foolishness as viewed
By the human spirit.

The Truth
Knows the heart
Of what matters most
Teaching day by day lessons.

So
If one learns from mistakes
The mistake is not in error
But a turning point
A type of signal.

So
The difference
Between weird and unique
Is the difference
Between bad and good
With being weird
As the act of demons
With being unique
As the act of the spirits.

So
The act
Of calling good
Bad and bad
Good is a deception.

To hate
Is part of life;
It happens
And is a weird gene
Planted in the earth of humankind.

To love, truly
Is a gift to humankind
Pointing the way
To the Life of Truth.

A butterfly
Yellow, plain but pretty
In its delicately bouncing
Dab in the air
Caught the eye of Captain Lee
And Chaplain Hawk watched it
Along with her
Both amused as it sat
On the boulder.

Turning to Chaplain Hawk
His face looking fatigued
After his grunt with the rock
She said, "Good thing
It didn't sit on that stone earlier
'Cause we never would have been
Able to move it, then."

Chaplain Hawk smiled, his shirt
Wet from sweat; yet,
The morning was cool.

Nodding,
He looked down at the ground
Noticing a fury of ants
Huge black ants crawling
On the ground, crawling
On his shoes, crawling
On Captain Lee's shoes.

He shook his legs.

She jumped away
And peevishly cried:

"Why weren't they here before?
They could have helped
With that raucous rock."

The task done
A rest taken, they continued
Their journey down the road.

The road was there, always there
Calling to the riders, touching
Their minds with mystery.

The Tweedledees all knew
The lure of the road; it was
Their lore, their love.

The road and a motorcycle
Are one;

The riders are along
For the joy of it.

As the morning grew later
The mountains showed their bones
Strong, powerful, majestic
And the wind carried their sensing
Through the trees on a wilderness road.

A sign.

A restaurant ahead.

Almost too late for breakfast.

With the late morning air
Growing thick and warmer
A breeze, gentle and kind
Wafted scents of autumn
Scents that opened the heart
To the eternity known to spaces
Far and deep within bone, within mind
And the Tweedledees
Began their descent
To the village of Stinky Creek.

It was a place
Of one gas station
One restaurant, one bar
Three buildings lying alone
At a crossroads

Where mountains lifted
Into the morning air
Where the sun broke
Through bulbous clouds
Where a circle
Of four or five vultures
Searched for carrion.

The buildings were older
But not decrepit.

The sun was bright
But not intrusive.

The vultures were on high
But close to hunger.

Parking before the restaurant
Shutting down the growl
Of their motors
The Tweedledees dismounted
Their hardware
And all noticed two young men
At the gas station, arguing.

They were standing
Nose to nose, eyeball to eyeball
Yelling loudly, waving their fists
Erratically
Into the autumn air
Digging their index fingers
Into each other's pride-filled chest
And the Tweedledees noticed them
And their hostilities
From across the street.

The Tweedledees filled
The restaurant

And a man took their food requests;
Another, an older man
Entered soon thereafter.

This older man of years
With a face of white whiskers
Was built solidly, his biceps
Still showing a flex of muscle
His chest chiseled
From years along ridges
Of these mountains
His waist, lean.

His eyes were clear
And a steely blue.

He ordered a burger
With raw onions and coffee.

When the older man
Received his food
He placed his rugged fists
On either side
Of his plate, looking up
with his eyes closed, tightly.

It was as if
The heavens in all their glory
Opened up to his soul
With the trumpets
Of ten thousand angels
Carrying his prayer
To The Unknown God
And it seemed as though
The day grew brighter
As though the earth trembled slightly
As though the room
Grew closer, more still, more quiet.

Some Tweedledees took note
While others never noticed;
Chaplain Hawk and Captain Lee
Looked on.

Tethered to a young boy
Of seven or eight years
Bouncing in the air
With each step he skipped
Two large balloons, one red, one blue
Followed him, as if
They were the patron saints
Of youth, guarding this youth
From the pronouncements of an age
That knew less of what matters most.

The boy stopped and stared
At the stand of motorcycles
In front of the restaurant.

The balloons bobbed in the air
Waiting patiently
For him to continue his romp.

He was blond haired
Serpentine-eyed, with a head shaped
With the suggestion of in-breeding
Common to this back-world
Of mountains and forests.

A single shotgun blast
Cracked through the air.

Across the street
At the gas station
One man lay on the ground
Splattered there
Against the ground, against the building

While the other man
Walked to his truck
Rather matter-of-factly
A weapon in his right hand
The argument settled;
Then, he slowly and carefully
Drove off, down the road.

The Tweedledees looked on.

The little boy resumed
Skipping down the road.

"Is someone
Going to call the police?"
Asked Captain Anna Meta Lee.

"Weeyall ain't got no
Powleese hee-ahh in Stinkie Creeek, mae-yam.
Weeyall ahr ahr own law hee-ah"
Said the man behind the counter.

The local who had prayed
Before his burger looked up
His eyes rolled into the back
Of his white-haired head;
Maybe there
He found some kind
Of a rationale.

After brunch, the Tweedledees
Refueled their motorcycles
Across the street at the gas station
Stepping carefully
Around the parts of the man
Who lost the argument.

"What are they going
To do with the body?"
Asked Captain Anna Meta Lee.

"Probably throw it
Out back for the wild pigs.
They eat everything:
Bones, flesh, teeth and all."
The old man answered
From across the way.

As the day drew
Into a lovely afternoon
The sun warm, gentle, friendly
They continued their ride.

CHAPTER 4: DEEPER INTO THERE

True or False:

The heart is to meaning

As The Unknown God is to language?

Then, it was
That Eagle Hawk's house
Was clean
But out of nowhere
Came a curse.

A demon
Seeing that all was
In order saw to it
That it would pursue
That curse
And the demon
Brought a plentitude
Of evil upon him.

In a warp
Of time and space
Eagle Hawk fell
Victim
Of this insidious evil
And being crumbled
Beneath the weight
Of the torment.

A grey stone face
Leered in a darkness
And a message
Followed
Written upon his soul.

This, it said
Was the head
Of The Unknown God.

Fallen through space and time
The demons tore
At Eagle Hawk's mind.

The line drawn
Between the possible
And what was there
Launched
A saber into the heart
Of substance
As demons
Gained control of his thoughts
Bending Truth
Into the mask of chaos.

Eagle Hawk became
A puppet
Tortured through days
And nights.

It was
That the religions
Of the world
Would wait their turn
To be of ultimate power.

With The Unknown God dead
The other gods shuffled
For dominance.

As a puppet for demons
They manipulated
Eagle Hawk's mind to see
The hidden meaning
Behind the writing
On the wall
When the message
Sent
Took his being
Into the depths
Of delirium.

It was
Through deceit that the demons
Ripped a man from his God.

A puppet master
Pulled the strings
Anchored in Eagle Hawk's mind
Leading him to a place
Of glass and concrete
With a floor
Tiled in a mosaic
Of quadrants.

There he laid
Before all the gods
All
Except The Unknown God.

Then space dissolved
The moment
Into one vision
After another.

His heart raced.

His mind collapsed.

His being spun
Across the quadrants
Of time and space
Until he found himself
Somewhere on a path
Through a woods.

It was a day
And a night, again
And again.

He was thirsty
But he was not
Allowed to drink.

The hot sun scorched
His tongue.

Then, it was
That Eagle Hawk
Found himself in Vietnam
During a period
Marked by the Sixties.

He was approaching
A rice paddy
When all hell broke loose.

Time shifted
Times and a half
As the logic and reason
Of being there
Fell before the actual
As perceived by Eagle Hawk.

He was both there
And not there
Caught in the pain
And anxiety
That dwelt with combat.

As the bullets
Hit their target
As his buddies dropped
From life
They were all
Torn apart by lead
Their eyes smoked by death
His face buried in the mud.

He tried to pray
To The Unknown God
In the name of The Word
But all he found
Was pain and death.

He cried out
For mercy but all
There was
Was a mouth full
Of mud and blood.

Then, time and space
Leaked out
Of the experiential
As the demons
Intensified his torment.

Eagle Hawk laid
In a bed
In a room
Beyond oblivion
And he felt something
Tugging at his feet.

It was a demonic
Puppet master pulling
Eagle Hawk into the second death
A place of no return
And he began to recite
The creed he had learned
As a child
That he knew by heart
But the demon stole
His confession of faith
Leaving a void
Followed by forlornness.

He passed out
Before the lake of fire
As a broken man.

Even his faith
Seemed to have
Left him
As he trembled
In hopelessness.

So
It was that Eagle Hawk
Took on the name
Of Legion
Because he had become
A mind of many voices
Tormented by demons
Tortured by demons
Until he was
A cripple robbed
Of his faith
In The Unknown God.

He learned
That in the lake of fire
There is no place
For mercy
No place for faith
No way of deliverance.

Time and times and a half
Spun in his mind
As his pursuit of Truth
Intensified.

Then
Although it was
An ordinary day

A day like any other
Eagle Hawk understood
That the ground
Of the extraordinary
Was concealed
In the province of the ordinary
That there was always room
For the extraordinary
Within the common
As if the times were leaves
Of a massive tree
Yet, unique
By each leaf's placement
In a panorama of light
Fulfilling its purpose
As one of many
Yet, never two precisely the same.

He thought of the common
As a window to beauty
A union of the breath of life
With the soul
Of what matters most
As the sun rose in its time
And later would set
The span
A daylight revealing an unknown
From darkness.

So
The day advanced
From the known
To the unknown
The Truth in being there
As a passage of space
Through time.

While in a deep vision
The very last thought
That he would have on this planet
Was imprinted on his brainstem.

Since then,
That imprint was reinforced
With every breath that he took
Onto his unconscious,
Each and every breath
Allowed and allowing.

Through a parabola of time
Eagle Hawk reached the moment.

So
All allowing
Strengthened that connection.

It is Scriptural.

The scene is Christ's crucifixion
When He turns to one
who dies with Him.

The last thought is,
"Today I shall see you in paradise."
With Eagle Hawk being
The figure of the thief
 Who was saved.

He hoped truly,
That it would be
His very last thought
Before he died.

Then
In a vision
His teacher visited him
To overcome
Time and space.

Then
Eagle Hawk listened
As his teacher spoke.

So
The most fundamental need
Is survival and its fight
Or flight reflex
While the seminal need is
Sexual responsiveness
Linked to procreation.

Thus, the life of the man
Is designed with all pain
As the trigger culminating
In the fight or flight reflex,
And all pleasure as the trigger
culminating in scintillating titillation
the tickling of a legacy;
In a sense, pain versus pleasure
Threat to survival
Versus sexual responsiveness
Are the yin and yang
Of being there.

These two needs form the nucleus
Of the body of the self
Determining behavior,
But only to a degree.

Dean C. Gardner

All other needs
Are as if the electrons
Spinning around this nucleus,
The appendages and digits
Of that body.

However, the need
That supersedes these needs is
To remain connected
To one's spiritual core.

The spiritual core is
As if the DNA of a man,
Determining the heart of character,
The very substance of the soul,
The aura of his being there.

To be disconnected
From one's spiritual core
Is the arch breach to one's existence,
A separation from one's purpose
That supersedes all
Other experiential phenomenon.

It is a point of disorientation
Confusion, chaos,
And ultimately despair;
Thus, one outlives oneself.

To reestablish the physical connection
Between the very last thought
A man has
Onto his brainstem
And the connection of a man
To his spiritual core,
First each breath that he takes
Must be controlled so that
The sympathetic

And parasympathetic nervous systems
Are engaged to maintain
The integrity of the person:
The more allowing the person is
The more the person
Conquers his pain,
The more
Thoroughly integrated he is
To his spiritual core.

All good neutralizes pain.

To one degree or another,
There is always pain;
It is part of the human condition.

Good must be applied
Externally and allowed internally.

Pain disconnects the spiritual core
From a man,
Unless it is established beyond
The pain threshold of this world.

When the spiritual core connection
Transcends this pain threshold
A person is free.

The purpose, in a sense,
For man in this life is
To prepare him for death.

When that preparation is finished,
He dies with his spiritual core
As the last impression of his being,
His true legacy.

As a spiritual man
Eagle Hawk displaced
The pain by reinforcing the good.

In this reality
To each person
There is the light of darkness
As well as the Light of light
Indwelling within him:
The light of darkness is evil
Dwelling within the person;
The Light of light is the good
Dwelling within the person.

The war of principalities
Is waged in the mind and heart
Of each person.

Some people form
The lost constituents
Damned for eternity
Into a lake of fire.

Some people form
The found flock
Of The Word
Bound for the Glory Road
Onto forevermore.

The Unknown God's will predestines
The damned constituents
To be slaves to despair
Outside and inside of linear time
Through a vertical column of time.

All are predestined
From a vertical column of time.

It is not for man to know truly
Who is a constituent
And who is of the flock;
That is determined by grace
Through faith
In The Word on Judgment Day.

The demons place evil toxins
Onto a person through the curse;
These evil toxins are worked out
Through the good
On the battlefield of the war
Of principalities.

As part of his training
A complete transference was made
Onto his enlistment
As a spiritual man
With the teacher's hands
Being his hands,
His limbs being
The limbs of the teacher
Until achieving a complete
Out-of-body experience
Through placing anchors
Within his person
And then setting triggers and cues
Onto being there.

Triggers are visual signs
While cues are verbal signs.

It is destiny
That determines
Anchors, triggers and cues
With a link to the brainstem.

By sensing
The Unknown God's heart,
All good
Works out evil toxins
Through the gentle touch
Of The Word
A type of laying of hands
That reconnects one
To one's spiritual core.

In Scripture death is described
In a variety of forms
From the bleakness
Of David's treatment
Of the hopeless grave
To Jesus' expression
Of death as sleep.

Taking Christ's metaphor of sleep
After departing from this world,
Is it possible that we enter a dream state
With a pleasurable dream as the room
Of The Unknown God's house
Where the Saints dwell,
And a ghoulish nightmare
As the dwelling place
For the unregenerate soul
A slave to suffering?

In the universes of possibility
There is only the world of Actuality
And that is Truth;
Here and now is the stage.

The Unknown God abounding
Throughout his form and substance
Was convincing Eagle Hawk that
Through the gentle touch,

Progress is made in his muscle,
His bone, his mind and his spirit.

It may even be a rebirth
Of the who that The Word
Wanted him to be.

What did the spirit of the age
Want him to do
To boost this progress?

What did he need to do to help
His self connect to his spiritual core?

In what ways could he be
More responsive to The Word?

When Eagle Hawk
Planted anchors
In his body, as The Word
Exercised his faith
Upon his form
With the trigger
Of the gentle touch and verbal cue
Set in time and beyond time
He was more responsive
To what matters most.

Eagle Hawk was convinced
That the more responsive he was
To The Word
The more connected
He shall become
And the healthier, more vital
His self shall be.

He saw the gentle touch
Through The Word
As preparation for service.

Through Eagle Hawk 's teacher
He had learned to project himself
From this four dimensional reality
Of the here and now,
To a two dimensional reality
(the transitional phase)
And into a one dimensional Actuality,
Which is the projection
Into the pure energy
Of a parabola of time.

From his study of Haiku
Along with a grounding in Truth,
He had learned the matter
Of juxtaposition and connectivity.

As the body records anchors
And through repetition of anchor,
Trigger and cue over time,
A pattern of neural pathways
Is formed
A body memory is imprinted,
The pattern growing
From the randomness of juxtaposition
To the precise and clear image desired
By the spiritual man
To see with the eye in the back
Of the mind.

As the image becomes
More clearly registered
In the mind, there is greater
And greater connectivity.

Thus, a channel is formed,
Culminating in fructification
That transcends space,

So
The actual can be resurrected
Whenever Eagle Hawk desired
Whatever dimension he dwells in
At any given time,
A type of sharing a beautiful
And wondrous dream
Ordained by The Unknown God.

If the teacher allows it to be so,
He was enabled to visit dreams
In the sleep state,
But he could only do so,
as directed by faith;
That is the first given
To dream visitation.

Of course
It was his teacher
That determined the dream
By setting anchors, triggers and cues,
The second given of dream visitation;
But of course, one cannot
Violate the law
Of The Unknown God;
The only other given.

When Eagle Hawk gained control
Of his connectedness
In linear time,
Dream visitation was accomplished;
That is what his teacher
Designed him to do.

Yes, believe it or not,
He was called a student,
Who learned to journey
To other's dreams
As service to The Word.

Eventually, whenever the teacher
Desired Eagle Hawk's attention,
Simply a thought would cue
an anchor in his brainstem:
Eventually all that needed to be done
Was for the teacher
To think that thought.

That is how Eagle Hawk
Was reconfigured.

Yes, one is led to the understanding
That The Word guided him to be
An instrument of the The Unknown God
Through dream visitation.

Eagle Hawk accepted that calling.

As faith removed the toxic anchors
With the gentle touch,
Progress was made.

So
along the way
Were the teacher
Who said things straight
And Eagle Hawk
With a war cry of blood
That expunged the root
Of the cancer
Spreading across the land
As what matters most
Was restored from sea
To shining sea.

That is how the teacher
As master of the rolling thunder
Taught Eagle Hawk to shoot;

Then
The golden valise
Of secrets was found
A wondrous gift.

However, there were puppet masters
With their plan
Of total universe destruction
The evil toxin spreading across
All dimensions of the actual.

Eagle Hawk
Through the integrated collective
Volunteered to head South
Where he met up with
Captain Anna Meta Lee
And her sister
Olivia from oblivion.

Together, these three
Followed The Word
And unbound the Prometheus
Of the human heart
Shoring up the leaks
In the integrated collective
That rainbow promise
Of ages past.

It was
That Grandpa Time was one
Of Eagle Hawk's favorite teachers.

CHAPTER 5: TOWARD TONGUES OF FIRE

True or False:

The accuser is to torturous persecution

As The Word is to merciful judgment?

In a distant place
Where all of time collided
With the nth degree of space
The silhouette of a Trumpet stood
His attention focused
Onto the nuances of a dawn to be
As the whence of being
Penetrated the hence of nothingness
And the sound of the unknown
Shook the bones
Of what matters most.

To know all
Is pathologically delusional;

To know enough
Starts with the knowledge
Of one's limitations
And continues endlessly
With a delicious smile
Of satisfaction.

To know best
Is the domain of The Word.

Around the look
Of that Trumpet's silhouette
From a forest of stars
Above most constellations
Grew the scent of a wolf
And the eyes of Olivia
From oblivion
Saw Truth with turquoise eyes
That were given to her
By the very first rising sun.

She was
In many mysterious ways
An archetype of Truth
With the turquoise orbs
Of her seeing
There to reveal the secrets
Knotted in the soul
Of this and any other universe
As the Trumpet's silhouette founded
The archetype of the seeker.

At the end
Of Olivia's dreams this night
Was the first tale
Of Bennie and the Wizard.

Bennie
Was a frog
Who was unlike any other frog
In the whole world.

While other frogs
Were busy croaking
At each other
Or eating worms and flies
Bennie would sing.

He sang
To the morning sun
As it peeped
Its head
Over the mountain top.

He sang to the trees
Or to the warm summer breeze.

He sang to the rabbits
Squirrels and bears;
It did not matter
To Bennie.

He sang to anybody
For any reason.

Life was a song worth singing
To Bennie
And that is what he cared
Most about.

On Bennie's birthday
The animals of the forest
Gave him a present.

"Could it be a ball? Could
It be a book
That told of buried treasure?

What could it be? What
Could it be?" sang Bennie.

Without a minute lost
Bennie opened the present.

It was not
A ball, or even a book.

It was a bright red bow tie.

Bennie
Was so happy;
He tried it on.

Ooooooohh,
What a good looking tie it was!

Bennie thanked all his friends
For the bow tie.

He thanked big Hank
The bear.

He thanked Bridget
The rabbit.

He thanked Archie
The opossum.

Bennie
Was so happy
With his new bow tie
That he sang
A song thanking all of his friends.

I thank you all
Big and small
For this beautiful bow tie.
It is much better
Than a worm or a fly.

I will wear it always
No matter where I go
Because it is from friends
Whose hearts make me glow.

One day
While Bennie was singing
A wizard came by.

"My, what a beautiful voice
You have."
The wizard said
"I bet you don't know
Dream Train!"

"I do. I do"
Said Bennie
And he began to sing.

Dream train, please carry me back.
Dream train, stay on the right track.
Stop when a sweet old lady hollers
Welcome, my dream train.

"Splendid!" said
The wizard.
"For that
I will grant you one wish."

Bennie was puzzled.

"What kind of wish
Will you grant? I can think
Of nothing I want or need."

The wizard was surprised.

In his travels
He had never found anyone
Who did not have
Something to wish for.

"I'll give you anything
Whatsoever." Said the wizard.

But Bennie
Could think of nothing.

"You can have
A pot of gold.
Would that not be nice?"
The wizard said.

"But, what would
I do with it? I think
Gold would be too heavy
To carry around." Said Bennie.

"I will give you
A cruise around the world.
You could see London and Paris.
And the pyramids
Are lovely this time of year.
Wouldn't you like that?"

"But, I never traveled much.
This
Is my home.
Why would I want
To go anywhere else?" Bennie said.

The wizard was stumped.

Bennie sat
And thought and thought.

He could not think
Of anything that he wanted
That he needed.

The wizard had never
Met anyone like Bennie.

They sat together
And thought and thought.

"Think
Of your wildest dreams . . .
All of the wonders in this world
I'll give them all to you." said the wizard.

Bennie jumped into the air.

"I've got it. I've got it!" sang out Bennie.

"What is it?" asked the wizard.

"Will you be my friend?" asked Bennie.

"Me?" cried out the wizard.

"I never had a friend before.
Sure!
I think that would be marvelous.
A friend . . . a friend, indeed."

And, that is how
The wizard
And Bennie the frog
Became friends.

True or False:

Mental illness is to seeking hidden meaning

As The Word is to grasping a vision?

COLLECTED EXPERIMENTS

The Test

Some time of not so long ago
he was an average student
at an average university in pursuit
of an average education;
he knew himself ignorant then
and he knew himself ignorant now –
thus, he concluded that some things
do not change.

He remembered that it was
final exam time in a
        philosophy course
that gave him an insight
into the magnitude of his folly.

The exam was three hours
        in duration
and all the students had
        the very same task:
to complete the writing
        of two essays.

First, blue-books were distributed
to each student; then,
a small yellow sheet of paper

with the two essay topics legible to all.

Essay 1: through argumentation,
prove that you exist.

Essay 2: through argumentation,
prove that you do NOT exist.

Certainly, all of the class could feel
the rise of the temperature
    in that June
sun-baked classroom, with the beige
of the blinds dangling limp
from the windows, not blocking out
the heat, but rather summoning it
all the more as a malevolence
defining the moment.

Of course, there were no fans,
no circulation present
    and as the students
composed their two statements,
each tapped a foot following
    the rhythm
of the drip of each other's sweat
onto the warped oak floor.

In the blinking of an eye, everyone
was done with both essays, the three hours
of each of their lives voided
into a hot June day.

With thankful hearts most students
evacuated the classroom
    with the hope that air
could be found somewhere.

A few students, however,
    stayed in the torment
of that oven, realizing
    their accomplishment
and that remnant blankly observed it
in silence, unnerved in their broil.

Each of their two essays proved
both sides equally true, equally valid
equally acceptable as fact.

They also understood
that if they had acquired the skill
to equally prove and disprove
        what is there,
they were equipped to do
the very same for what is not there.

Thus, all of the remnant accepted
that since none had a reason
to trust anything he or she thought
there was no plausible reason
to trust the thoughts of anyone else.

So the remnant sat there
        puzzled in pits
of their own perspiration,
        victims of their own minds,
wondering where to go to from there.

Some of the remnant never left
that June heat; some are there still.

As it is written:
"I will destroy the wisdom of the wise;
the intelligence of the intelligent I will frustrate."

The Stalking

Ponderous and powerful
the grizzly moves its mass
as whole trees yield
to its might,
as its paws swipe
through the thickets,
as its jaws, heavy with teeth
snap and snarl at the wind
that carries your scent
to its dark nostrils –
yet, you walk
in the sprinkling of sunlight
through the forest
where fern and flower
bloom radiantly, while peace
covers you like a heavenly blossom
in a garden of joy.

To dedicate your life to an art form
to live the pain of so many, many years –
then, to let the Lord Almighty take your hand
and deliver you to peace and to joy.

As it is written: "Of making many books there
is no end, and much study wearies the body."

Busy in their flight
for food for family, the little juncos

dart across the green canopy,
their efforts rewarded
by a brood of nestlings
fragile in their lie, as you
recline upon a knoll
listening to their twitter
watching their flit, and the sun
round and golden, speaks
with warmth in deep sweeps of silence –
yet, the grizzly bristles
across the bush
brutal in its tracks toward
your scent.

It is that there never is a step in your
journey through this life that you were ever
alone or forsaken because the Lord was
protecting you from the wilds of the world.

As it is written: "God is our refuge
and strength, an ever-present help
in trouble. Therefore we will not fear,
though the earth give way and the mountains
fall into the heart of the sea."

Approaching ever so closely
the grizzly stood on its hind legs
thrashed about in the brush
disturbing the juncos
which attacked the grizzly's eyes,
pecked them out in a fury of flurries,
as blood streamed down
the grizzly's face, as the juncos' frenzy
blinded the grizzly,
and you stirred, alarmed at the terror
a hand breath away –
yet, the grizzly's jagged jaws
snapped blindly as it was consumed
by its own darkness
laced with the taste of its own blood.

Although the world wages a ruthless war
against you with fires in torrents of terror,
sing praises to our Mighty God with thanks
and rejoice in His bountiful blessings.

As it is written: "The teaching of the wise
is a fountain of life, turning a man
from the snares of death."

Not long thereafter,
you shall return
to that knoll in the forest
as the sunlight spreads softness
through the green
as the juncos flit about
still feeding their young
as the land awakens with life and joy –
yet, not too far away the carcass
of the grizzly lies motionless
in its death,
as flies crawl through the hollows
of its eyes, as maggots fill its belly,
and you shall know once again
that the Lord is with you.

As it is written: "Then Samuel said,
'Speak, for your servant is listening.'"

Soup du Jour

It was not
a copper kettle
handmade in the hills
of Bohemia
by a gypsy tinker
with a lame horse
not a cauldron
where spirits moved around
with wings of crystalline magic
but the common kettle
of contemporary alloy
a shiny pot
glowing on the stove.

It was not
the dew swabbed
from ten thousand
white tail buck antlers
not the sweet waters
that rushed down
the Andean mountain side
not the brackish waters
where the deep of the sea
washes the fertile crescent
but it was
the water from the faucet
cool and wet in its colorlessness.

Dean C. Gardner

The onion was red
and the size of a lumberjack's fist.

The garlic was fresh
minced and in ample portion.

Salt and pepper flanked
the oregano
with a portion of spinach and carrots.

Two chicken thighs
had thawed
by the side of the sink
the skin a rich yellow
the meat an off pink
the bone concealed.

The crimson
of the poinsettia
looked on as if to see
the curiosity.

What was there
was there
nothing more, nothing less.

The water boiled
frothing with garlic
salt, pepper, oregano
spinach and carrots.

The red onion danced
between bubbles of water
wild with steam.

Then the thighs
found home in the pot.

With the heat turned down
into a gentle simmer
it was time
for a rich perfume
to envelope the room
as time marked the moment
with icicles dangling
from the window eve.

The poinsettia
captivated by the fragrance
blushed.

The room glowed
into evening.

It was a soup
of magnificent design
poured over a bed
of whole grain noodle
a meal that spoke
with a thankful tongue
into the darkness.

As it is written:
"and the truth
shall set you free."

The Seed of Appearance

The oak, a tree towering into
the above with limb upon limb
more green than the word green
but not more alive than the breath
in the vitals of the living in it,
has grown into being itself
and before the green tree
a man equally green lingers in
a greener quiet until now, that moment
when he is the language of his being
as the wind from time under and through
stirs him toward infinite possibility.

Just as the oak appears before
his eyes, the word "oak" appears
before the seeing of his substance
as more of a myth than the thing
itself – yet, he speaks that word
as if he had always owned it, although
all words seem to penetrate the masks
in being there, are beyond the self, and are lodged
in the very meat of what is the soul.

However, it is written, "In the beginning
was the Word, and the Word was with God,
and the Word was God."

Oh mighty oak, if this man cloaked
in a greener quiet from time under
and through, strikes a match to your hide
and flames consume you, your speechless
pride will ride through the winds
into time past, and the clouds
that knew your green crown
will carry your ash to visions
far beyond his eyes – yet
in your living you are more
than the magnitude of your life,
the oak that stands tall being the seed
of your mystery within the mind,
the very oak of what is there.

If a thing is only what it appears to be,
it has no meaning in and by itself
but merely a relativity as determined
by the subject who perceives it.

As language becomes immersed
        with the image
infused within itself, while the oak
of trees leaps
into the sky with its roots pulling the earth
into the heavens
and while the soul of this green man
of quiet proceeds
out of the indwelling of the Holy Spirit
and not by his conceiving himself out
of his own
utter nothingness, as the oak by itself cannot
believe its being into form and substance,
tall and green,
sturdy and leafy, more there than not
the two together climb out of themselves
attached with an umbilical cord to the forever.

Language, indeed, is the vital surfacing
    of the spirit
between time under and time through,
that vertical
column of time encompassing the
living moment
which defines itself as the finite toward
the infinite.

What he sees as there is only
the trace of being and not the heart of its form
as what it is grows into its living there,
a speaking into substance as if an archeology
of horizons beyond sensibility, as the oak speaks
as the cross of the living Christ,
as it reaches through a parabola of time,
and the man of green finds his own image
hanging upon this life baring oak
with both their roots entwined.

As it is written, "Now we see but a poor
reflection; then we shall see face to face.
Now I know in part; then I shall know
fully, even as I am fully known."

Suspended beyond the living present,
he is continuously becoming
who he is through a believing in
and under the Word's passion, simultaneously –
yet, the who that he has become
can only be viewed from the no longer,
from beyond the image of himself;
consequently,
he is always that which is outside of his grasp,
as the oak that he sees is more
than it appears.

Try as one will, transcendence always eludes
being, as self is forever buried by the moment
with no take into the eternal, unless who
one is grows into a beyond one's own possibility.

Although he is not the oak
although he becomes his own crucifixion
on that mystery tree –
both live inside of him
their bodies deep within his mind
as he becomes something other
than the who that he was –
yet the same soul
and he pronounces this
word as the seed of the everlasting.

Consequently, words are amorphous creatures
finding their way to understanding
through the rhythm of inner spaces of heart
and tongue and other such universes
to dwell as faith, the sustenance of the soul.

For the Christ said, "I tell you the truth,
if a man keeps my word, he will never see death."

The Interior Other

As he looked into the looking glass he
understood he could not get passed the image
in his mind of what he knew of himself
because the mirror was merely one more
distortion of what he was before his substance.

He knew to himself, he was taller and leaner
than what was there. To him his eyes
were truer in color, his nose less arched,
and his lips more even than what was there.
He knew to himself there was a distinctive look
about his chin, a specific, yet indefinable prowess
about his forehead and the mark of meaning
to the mole on his left cheek
but he believed the mirror could not
possibly hold such a view of him.

With the world brimming with billions of people
he told himself that he was like no one else but
he understood that his was the heart true
to all men.

As it is written: "The Lord God formed the man
from the dust of the ground and breathed
into his nostrils the breath of life, and the man
became a living being."

In his eyes, he was the vision
behind the appearance, the soul
beneath the skin, the bone
of mountains holding truth to the light
and the muscle in the heart of the land –
    all such
things beyond the knowledge of mirrors.

Not being the common man
or the ordinary man, but also
not being the "special" man either,
he stood above himself into a dawn
of years far passed his time rocked age
as the sun glistened on his shoulder
as the wind tossed about his locks –
yet, he could never be seen as the observer
willed but only as he was with the color
of his mind mapping the metaphysical.

He walked along with the moon in silence
seeing his shadow follow along faithfully
while the night was painted with stars in dazzle
while his heart dissolved in the thick
of his breath
and he knew tomorrow could bring
no greater truth than what was already there.

There was a confidence in His eyes
without a trace of arrogance,
a certain depth to the line of His jaw
without a touch of the intimidating,
a graceful gentleness to His smile
without a tinge of sarcasm
and all whom He met found this
in Him and more as His measure
was truly greater than what they dreamed –
yet, He knew that everywhere it always
was already there while tomorrow would slip
through their fingers and yesterday
only could remain their constant grief.

He became himself through the steel
of the everlasting and the brass of the forever
with His soul as the metal of the moment;
then, He was of a multitude of geometries
into the beyond.

He was the doctrine of the landscape,
the physics of what it meant to be
and He was a soul in the world
but not a soul of the world. His image
was the vision beyond the soul.

As it is written: "Before I was formed
in my mother's womb, you knew me."

However, what made Him larger than life
and more than any looking glass could tell
was the vastness of His own suffering
the encompassing space of His own pain
as well as the blood of His self-sacrifice.

It was not only that He suffered, but the way
He endured his suffering. It was not
only that He had pain, but the way He triumphed
over it. Each day He awoke with devotion
to do the work of the Father
and each night He slept with thanksgiving.

In His air there was a calm.

To know Him as He truly is, is to receive
a transfusion of an inner universe, seeing who we
truly are, reaching for what we could be,
venturing
through the door behind the mind of forever.

To see Him is not to find distance
but to feel closeness, to not feel
the cold matter of an object but to fathom
the pulse of peace, to not face alienation
but to share in the indwelling of the Spirit.

As it is written: "He had no beauty or majesty
to attract us to him, nothing in his appearance
that we should desire him. He was despised
and rejected by men, a man of sorrows,
and familiar with suffering."

Thanksgiving Paradox

As the family gathers about the table round,
and the talk is of old times when we were so little
with the lime cream cheese gelatin belly up
that Mom always makes in a yellow orchid bowl
filling spoon after spoon just as it had
for so many years past, it is a Thanksgiving dinner
with more than turkey, more than warm looks
with a flame flickering in the eyes but less
    than our reaching
that brings a look of gentleness to the moment
with a deep vision of peace – yet,
    with a wink of wanting.

Although there is enough time to do
anything and everything, yet live still,
without a mind to carry through the day
but with heart enough to be burdened
as the thorns of wild thickets,
gray with frost, scrape and scratch
the sides of our minds, red, raw and festering,
each twist of the clock brings us that much
closer to being no more, as we fill the house
with the fullness of a single voice in tune
with the ceaseless celebration of our souls.

As it is written, "I waited patiently for the Lord;
He turned to me and heard my cry.
He lifted me out of the slimy pit, out of the mud
and mire; He set my feet on a rock and gave me
a firm place to stand. He put a new song in my mouth,
a hymn of praise to our God."

Wearisome is the sky with its impenetrable gray,
stagnant and stationary and vast,
more as a thick stone lid separating us
from forever, concealing the beyond
and muffling the trumpets of the heavens
than a void of vapors moved by a whim of physics
as the chill creaking through the spine
from a reckless wind cracks the marrow,
and the fingers curl and throb from the cold –
yet, it is not another hollow thud of a day
in November but the melody of a moment
with tender talk, that gentle sway of gentler spirits
since out there is not in here and we gather,
a bouquet of laughter and chatter,
a family flourishing in its blooms of care
as we give thanks for our hopes
for our dreams, and the very breath of our souls
even while beneath this gray death.

For Jesus, the Christ said, "Come to me, all
you who are weary and burdened, and I will give you
rest. Take my yoke upon you and learn from me,
for I am gentle and humble in heart, and you will
find rest for your souls. For my yoke is easy
and my burden is light."

As our time splashes from the table and soaks
our souls, the only way through the wall
is to pound our hearts against it, as His light
bathes these bodies through a glistening of smiles
with a twinkle shimmering boldly in the eyes,
that feel of a family bursting through the barriers
of being as the emptiness of our existence
is filled by God's love.

Beneath the gray sky, that death of neutered light
that smothers each breath and fills the lungs
with hungry gray worms, we find in the wreckage
of November weather a home in a house of hope
as a heavy foreboding shoots holes through our hearts,
and the fingers of the trees hold their brittle bones
to a body of interminable grayness, as we drink
from this dim well of light that seems less
than a leakage of time and more of a tangle
with the terminal gray of a dreary dream –
yet, awake – we dwell in the hope of our lives
with a very true touch of the forever.

Although the shadows, shapes and shades
of time, ponderous and powerful,
move from the face of the clock
to wear upon our souls thinner and thinner,
we chime victorious with our hands reaching
between us, as we grasp
our own inalienable everlasting with thanksgiving.

For it is written, "I will extol the Lord at all times;
His praise will always be on my lips. My soul
will boast in the Lord; let the afflicted hear
and rejoice. Glorify the Lord with me; let us exalt
his name together.

Launched out of Folly

He remembered
the forest thick with ferns
the young archeopteryx
bathing in a wealth of light
on a log grown green with moss.

The air was fertile and rich
with the smell of dawn
rising from the earth.

Light gathered in the sky
a golden hue
penetrating deeply
into the forest
as he looked and listened
for sounds of birds.

Falling from high above
the trill of a red-eyed vireo
its overture
to a day
more than an entrance
into the glossy pages
of forever.

He remembered not moving
not making a sound
as the rustle
of a nut hatch
caught his eye
it feeding its young
with speckled insects

How careful it was
that the wide mouths
found food.

How busy it was
tending to the tiny puffs
of feathers.

Off in the distance
across a stretch
flecked with golden light
a black bear stirred
as it foraged
hungry before the sleepy heat
of the day.

He remembered
that he did not think
but simply launched himself
charging the bear
yelling inscrutable sounds
and thrashing
through the forest green.

The bear did not rear
but sped off
to avoid confrontation.

They asked him
why he charged the bear
and he remembered
he did not know;
it was merely what he did.

As it is written:
"I have known madness
and I have known folly."

It was in him to do.

Had it been
a she-bear with cubs
it would have reared.

Confrontation
would have been inevitable

A she-bear with cubs
would have torn him apart..

As it is written:
"The Lord is my salvation."

Autumnal Awe

To look upon the mirror of the sky
where we and our kingdoms are absent,
that very blue, and see beyond it
into the vast reaches of space
witnessing the unblemished truth
of what is there as more clearly a mystery
than a discerning eye tells, as the depth
of its fathoms grows greater with us,
we at the bottom of eternity,
while a hawk hovers
up high, unbound and free, speaking
for the liberation of the soul from the physics
of being, of our pride, of our folly.

As the sun sends a universe of breath
through the boughs of a verdant pine
into the trembling muscle of the earth –
that sensation beyond substance,
that view beneath the vision,
that image before the understanding –
yet, to capture the rapture of that idea
with words as if we could hold them
brings to wonder where the trees
get their gold, as summer slips
a longing look over an autumn shoulder
that turned too soon
while winter approaches
with quickened strides
through a swirling wind
with an early chill,
as time spins silently
in its dervish where only mysteries
within being there light
through the passages
of a mind beneath the arc of the sun
and we are a speck there,
to vanish in a blink.

Marveling at the mysteries
of the moment beneath time
beyond the linearity
of any before or some after
as the image of the everlasting
is riveted into the eyes,
the mind sees only blue
in the deep crystal of space;
then, we can only marvel
through the clouds of our selves.

As it is written, "Therefore, the Lord himself will
give you a sign: The virgin will be with child
and will give birth to a son, and will call him
Immanuel."

Since we cannot touch the blue
of the sky, that clearer blue,
that purer blue, we feel it in our hearts
much like a firm handshake or a gentle pat
on the back is felt, thinking that we
understand it as it is, that we can trust it,
that it is there as it was before and will be
forevermore, remembering us who wonder
as if it mattered; yet, these mysteries present
opacities in the mind as groans fill the deep
of a soul that wanders beneath the sky
with an eternity emptying itself between
the heartbeats of the fullness of time
while the hawk configures the geometry
of being and nothingness with a form
near enough to see but far beyond our grasp,
and we gather what we are from the body
of our deeds as we yearn to escape from our bones,
as we measure the magnitude of our short falls,
as we marvel through the vapors of our selves
as our thoughts disappear into the quiet of light.

While awe lifts from the face of things
the scarlet mask that covers all truths,
the more we think, the less we know
the more we feel, the less we are
the more we do, the less there is
as the hourglass measures our losses,
the stuff men are made of, our futile pains.

As the Messiah hung upon a cross,
He said regarding our debt to God,
"It is finished."

A few steps before now,
as if unlike any
other moment of the day
when what was there
seemed more as loose ends dangling
out of somewhere,
the air filled suddenly
with the feel of an autumnal rain,
though the sky was high and clear
as the leaves spiraled into the earth
as the hawk cut circles in the blue –
yet, a damp chill buckled the knuckles
and disjointed the knees but only a mist
drifted cold
across the back then, when the heart dreamed
between meadows of clover and hills
of ice, the before and the after, while being
here was one more sleight of mind,
and we walked blind with our assumptions
to be stilled by the stand of eternity.

Behind the eyes in a look of being where
our faith is the only prelude to a beyond,
the mind catches the reflection
of a heart's song
echoing back and forth across distant skies.

Seeing the light that is called forth
from the very ends of time and space,
we feel the embrace of being here
where leaves dry and lazy find a home
on the street corner, as we leave our mark
in the concrete, shadows of footsteps
to eternity –
yet, we know the face of the moment
as a stumbling between what is seen
and what is there as these mysteries stagger
the soul.

For it is written: "Then I saw a new heaven
and a new earth, for the first heaven and the
first earth had passed away, and there was no
longer any sea. I saw the Holy City, the new
Jerusalem coming down out of heaven
from God, prepared as a bride beautifully
dressed for her husband."

Yes, our only hope is in the resurrection,
through Christ Jesus, our Lord and our Savior.

Nightly News

The flicker
of the screen
displays
the carnage
of tens of thousands
in yet another war
where the rape
and murder
of man, woman and child
are merely
a way of life –
and all
the grim atrocity
blossoms
in living color.

A flash to the newscasters reveals banter
about the weather – too hot, too cold,
too much precipitation, or not enough
as inane smiles bounce back and forth.

Jesus said, "When you hear of wars
and revolutions, do not be frightened.
these things must happen first,
but the end will not come right away."

Dean C. Gardner

An earthquake
with its pummeled
human flesh,
a fire
in a local home
with the hopes
of a family
burned
beyond recognition,
a murder
of a twelve year old
by a stray bullet
through the face –
and all
the grim atrocities
blossom
in living color.

Then to a commercial about toilet paper,
another one about the new car we all want,
an ad about untimely death protection,
as well as a blurb on the HIV
and safe sex.

Jesus said, "Nation will rise against nation,
and kingdom against kingdom. There will be
great earthquakes, famines and pestilence
in various places, and fearful events
and great signs from heaven."

A special report
follows
on smoking:
how it has
murdered
millions of Americans,
how cigarette manufacturers
are fighting
the people
in court
while peddling
their lethal vice to youth
and the anatomy
of lung cancer
blooms
on the screen
in living color.

The senses dead. Sensibility dead. We
gather around the kitchen table, bow
our heads and pray for our good fortune
to continue as life pours down the tube.

Jesus said, "Be careful, or your hearts
will be weighed down with dissipation,
drunkenness and the anxieties of life,
and that day will close on you unexpectedly
like a trap. For it will come upon all those
on the face of the whole earth. Be always
on the watch, and pray that you may be
able to escape all that is about to happen,
and that you may be able to stand
before the Son of Man."

Rainbow

Two by two they went
as the round top
of the universe dropped
beneath the stretches of reason –
yet, with uncertain knowledge
we look backward in disbelief,
as if we, on our own, could
form actual truths
out of stuff that we conjure
through the darkness
in our hearts, as if we
could bring a dawn
of dreams and visions
with the manipulation of our digits
and the end closed
upon the beginning
of the deepest rain.

We have become the shadows
in our own darkness, surrendering
our eyes for one more look
upon the blind pantomime of being
less than thoughts could configure.

Yet, it is written, "Let us make
man in our image, in our likeness,
and let them rule over the fish
of the sea and the birds of the air,
over the livestock, over all the earth,
and over all the creatures
that move along the ground."

Deeper the waters rose
to the very stars
as a trace of a thought walked
through silent breaks that only clouds
could construct, while the figures
of the idols we worshiped,
the work of our hands
and our preoccupation with our doings,
became a millstone sinking
us in an ever deepening abyss –
yet, we followed
our own way, stumbling
through our ineptitude
with calculated precision
as if we knew better than truth
and the waters rose.

Brother, do you hear the wind and the rain?
Sister, can you feel the fire through your tears?
Was there ever a yesterday as this moment
caught in the crypt of our own rebellion?

Jesus said, "Just as it was in the days
of Noah, so also will it be in the days
of the Son of Man. People were eating,
drinking, marrying and being given in marriage
up to the day Noah entered the ark. Then
the flood came and destroyed them all."

Tumbling from horizon
to horizon, the clouds unleashed
their bark of rain –
yet, we have forgotten
the roundness of the sun
as if our bustling could awaken
within us a new joy
much like eating a forbidden fruit
and choking on it, while wild thunder
passes upon us with triumph
as we quiver faint from our scurrying.

Where is the forever in your own breath
as you breathe your last moment in this?
And, when will you grasp the only reason
you were born at this awkward convenience?

As it is written, "But as for you
who forsake the Lord
and forget my holy mountain,
who spread a table for Fortune
and fill bowls of mixed wine for Destiny,
I will destine you for the sword,
and you will all bend down for the slaughter;
for I called but you did not answer,
I spoke but you did not listen.
You did evil in my sight
And chose what displeases me."

Although forty days and forty nights
is too long to tread water
while half a century
with grief raging through each year
is not long enough, as if
never ending is our despair,
ceaseless is our toil,
and constant is the hold
of futility upon us –
yet, our limbs, feeble,
dangle void of the blood
that we knew as our own
while our hearts pound death
into our bodies of decay
and our minds ignore our mortality.

Why we do not look
to the promise for the human soul,
why we choose our own blindness
rather than the eternal vision,
why we trust our senseless constructions
rather than the truth of Scriptural facts,
why we busy ourselves
with mindless mental fidgeting
and willfully forget what matters most,
remain the being beneath our breath –
yet, there is a rainbow.

The Simple Facts

Welcome to the Age of Disinformation, a time
when man murdered truth, where the people
cannot trust government because politicians
cannot resist the temptations of their power.

Curious: some things are what they are
irrespective of whether we understand them.

Song sparrow!
Your brain so small,
the size of a pea –
yet, you know how to fly
and can carry a tune . . .
Impossible!

To submit to the integrity of a revealed truth
is to transcend the reality of consciousness,
entering that sublime vertical column of time
where the self rejoices in merging
with the actual.

Prior to his crucifixion,
Jesus was asked by Governor Pilate,
"What is truth?"

Welcome to the Age of Disinformation, a time
when man murdered truth, where the people
cannot trust business because capitalism
is motivated by the pursuit of profit
and human greed.

Curious: some things mean what they say
and say what they mean irrespective
of whether we heed what is said.

Ant!
Your stomach so small,
the size of a grain of sand –
yet, you hunger and thirst,
visiting the same pantry
that I do . . .
Unthinkable!

For self to see consciousness as the other,
infuses truth into the soul, transcending
what we are and leaving far behind
the limitations of any and all reality.

As it is written, "What profits a man
if he gains the whole world,
but loses his own soul?"

Welcome to the Age of Disinformation, a time
when man murdered truth, where the people
cannot trust the media because the press
is motivated by special interests
and sensationalism.

Curious: being wrong knows no limits;
based on false information, a thousand people
can be wrong as easily as only one.

Dean C. Gardner

Mighty oak!
You stand so tall,
having no heart
to your limbs,
or within your upright body –
yet, I take it as an act
of kindness that you give
me cool from the summer sun . . .
Unimaginable!

Only through the indwelling of the substance
of a truth can the invisible be actualized
and the enslaving limitations of being there
be opened into an exercise of freedom.

Jesus said to the unbelievers responsible
for misinforming the people "You belong
to your father, the devil, and you want
to carry out your father's desire.
He was a murderer from the beginning,
not holding to the truth, for there is
no truth in him. When he lies, he speaks
his native language, for he is a liar
and the father of lies."

Welcome to the Age of Disinformation, a time
when man murdered truth, where the people
cannot trust themselves because
social engineers
have programmed them to be dull minded.

Curious: truth does not depend
on a consensus
or an expert opinion; truth is its own testimony.

Sky!
You are so purely blue,
more so than the blue guitar
and by far deeper
than mere feelings or thoughts –
yet, you give me air to breathe,
space to grow in
and something to look up to . . .
Unfathomable!

To accept one's very own limitations,
to merge with truth, the always already
significant, is to bring breath into the soul
and soar on the eternal wings of the beyond.

For it is written, "The wrath of God
is being revealed from heaven
against all the godlessness and wickedness
of men who suppress the truth
by their wickedness, since what may be
known about God is plain to them,
because God has made it plain to them."

A Chill Speaks

With all desire for life dead and with no
desire for death, his breath labors
in the veritable void of his being,
he, a man of grievous opacity
to his own self – yet, where there is
faith there is hope.

Although the frozen branches speak
with creaks and cracks in the wind,
and a chill snaps with wild snarls
through the shiver of frosted
pine cones as the grass grows
more dead under a shroud of snow
hopeless in the howl of winter,
cold bones draw dreams of being
somewhere else amid tulips
and green meadows with a sun,
radiant, bringing warmth to earth,
as a cup of coffee steams
through a dim December dawn
while the little gray squirrel
twitched in an open grave of snow –
yet, distance grows near with your touch.

Although with words we can prove
that you and you and you never existed,
Peter said to Jesus, "You are the Christ,
the Son of the Living God."

Curious: how the door is there to close,
to open, and to pass through to somewhere.

Last night as the cold strangled
silence out of winter's screech
when he dropped in a bed
of dying dreams with the throb
and ache of ages gnashing
his body of dull dry bones
he closed his eyes to life
for a final sleep to come
with nothing closer than the darkness
and its impenetrable feel
that grabbed the throat
holding his wind breathless
because darkness like death
with its shroud of madness
with its thick tyranny of a dense dread
snuffed out being –
yet, there was the hope that he would
awaken to a new day and a dawn
bringing the light and life
while the little gray squirrel
stiffens at the roadside and a blanket
of winter white covers its blood
and the fragrance of your face
embraced him with a warming feel.

Although we don't know for sure
that the table is there when we leave
the kitchen, Jesus said: "I tell you
the truth, whoever hears my word
and believes him who sent me has
eternal life and will not be condemned;
he has crossed over from death to life."

Curious: how the window is there
to look through to what is outside
while all that is there slowly passes away.

It is that the brutality of daylight reveals
the squalor of reality's decline,
the imperfections of a world
gone out of whack where form
juts out into formless space
as life overflows with random acts
of madness, where things appear, then drop
from view as if they never were,
as the blight of being there intrudes
on a quiet soul with stark images
as if objects were designed to offend
and attack and destroy sensibility –
yet, there is rest for the weary as the sunlight
filters through the clouds
and a simple peace is there
that surpasses understanding
as the rising steam of a cup of coffee
carries thoughts through a tranquil time
as the cold wind covers the darkness growing
across the face of the dead gray squirrel
and your lovely eyes sparkle
from the depths in a heart of faith.

Although some may scoff or malign
His Holy Name and berate Him
with fearsome disdain and disgust,
or belittle His Glory, Jesus said: "Forgive
them Lord for they know not what they do."

Curious: how the wall is there
to pound one's head against it,
so one may gain understanding.

Whether it is the cold of another
winter or the despair in another dark night,
or the brutal glare of another lighted day,
there is a home of many mansions,
a place of shelter from the atrocities
that wrestle away our life –
for there we find everlasting peace,
for there we find eternal joy,
for there we find a final rest
and the blood of the little gray squirrel,
frozen in a drift of time and snow
that is not unlike this world
lying in the waste of its age, is left buried
in the snows of forever – yet, we live
in the quiet folds of the Lamb of God,
as a cup of coffee awakens a new day
and your smile grows love into his eyes.

Curious: how the stars are there
to wonder at in our darkness.

Just a Child

From a tenement roof
in a summer's night,
thick and deep,
while quiet slipped
a sleepy eye,
Bobbie Ashley,
of all ten years,
climbed to the roof
to watch the moon chase
the stars in a starry night.

No one should know the back snapping
of poverty
because all and each are born beneath
the same sun,
and no one should be torn by the hooks
of violence
because all stand in the line for our turn
with death.

Perched
on a fire escape,
the geraniums orderly
and controlled,
Bobbie dreamed
of golden wings
spread across
a golden valley
fed by crystal streams,
and of a city
at peace
in a land of dignity.

To dream of truth flowing freely in the air
between the outstretched arms
of moon beams
and the fist-pounding glare of the street lights
takes a certain breed of an indefinable
courage.

What jewel,
robust yet immaculate,
this moon
as it hovered above
in its testimony
of pure silence –
to Bobbie Ashley
it held the promise
that only a child
could understand truly
but would never tell
those secrets
of the moon written
upon a child's heart.

If we do not care for the child with us,
if we do not protect our sons and daughters
from that evil, gouging out the heart from life,
how soundly do we sleep and why rise
to the day?

Upon the rooftop
Bobbie stood tall,
all ten years,
as time for a child
had not begun
its way
of isolation and calamity,
as Bobbie Ashley
soared
from galaxy to galaxy,
the night in a hush.

Even in poverty, the heart can triumph
as the moon is there for all to wonder,
and the sun rises for the poor and rich alike,
as each day is a treasure for all to keep.

The child
never heard
the hammer whack
although Bobbie Ashley
dropped with a thud;
it was a bullet
finding its place
through the heart
of a dream,
a child wrapped
in the warmth
of a summer night
and felled
by a drive-by shot.

What greater joy than a good-hearted child,
as the poison seeps in from this
foul-faced world,
and who could hold the hands of time true,
as what has passed and what is past is
cast aside?

And the Lord has said, "Will the one
who contends with the Almighty correct him?
Let him who accuses God answer him!"

It was not
the blood-stained pajamas,
the tears
of Mrs. Ashley
over Bobbie's body
growing colder,
or the peal
of sirens
in the starry night,
but it was
a winter later,
standing at the grave
of a child
who dared to dream
by the glow of the moon
wondering simply . . .
Why, why . . .

As the Lord has said, "For my thoughts
are not your thoughts, neither are your ways
My ways. As the heavens are higher than the
earth
so are my ways higher than your ways
and my thoughts than your thoughts."

The Juror

Up thirty-two granite stairs and down
countless marble halls leading to a court room
of deep oak and gas chamber green,
thirteen people gathered together
with nothing more in common than being there
and we were to decide whether a man
goes free
or spends the rest of his natural life
behind bars.

How the potential for truth colors factual reality
when the tedium of word upon word
piles higher and higher in the lows
of a stiff chair, as the fullness of the bladder
penetrates each twist to the listening ear
and the heavy, warm air collapses the mind.

To separate the idea of innocence
from that transparent look of guilt,
as the defendant fidgeted with his fingers
as his attorney chased his nose
through the ever stiffening air, took more
than the silence of a mind caught
between the thought of murder and the act
of crushing someone's skull with an iron pipe
although the thirteen of us sat listening
as if that distance could be measured
with eyes focused only on verifiable facts.

Murder: a violent beast in the muscle
of a man, its heart as his own.

As it is written, "He who is without sin,
cast the first stone."

It is not a question of the color
of the wall, whether green, blue or gray,
because as the sun moves and shadows grow
its appearance changes. It is not a question
of the wall being there for us to see and touch
for ourselves by our own senses, because
we cannot
resurrect that experience. However, it is
a matter of believing those who say
that they saw the wall, felt the wall,
measured it in the eye of the idea
of what a wall truly means and swear
that without a doubt, it was a wall that
was there.

But when one swears that the wall
was there while another swears
that it was not, then the question becomes
who we should believe regarding the wall.

Of course, the wall cannot be both
there and not there at the same time.

With long, drooping ears and eyes
too far apart,
with thinning hair and a graying
pencil mustache
while wearing a shirt that hung plaid over
his shoulders and pants that dragged
on the floor
he was a witness of slow, deliberate speech
who justified himself by the point
of his hooked nose.

According to him, the wall was there.

With the curves of her body singing youth
as her eyes sparkled brightly and bangles
jangled as she directed the air with quick
and constant ellipses flowing from her finger tips
she spoke a glow of words that flowed
from her heart
but there was a tear in the corner of her voice.

According to her, the wall was not there.

As witness after witness was weighed
in scales,
as prosecutor and defense whined and wailed
as word upon word numbed the brain
as hours wore the days painfully in needling
gray stripes,
we sat and listened, the ornaments of justice.

In a world where everyone lies some
of the time,
where everyone has an agenda
and everyone has
a motive, this was the place for discerning
the truth.

As it is written, "All have sinned
And fall short of the glory of God."

The room grew smaller, closing in around us
and our tempers shortened with the air sticky
and thick while nine of us saw what we heard
as guilt, three of us felt reasonable doubt
and a flock of flies feasted on our lunch.

Some spoke, some listened while others
stared with their arms folded, their minds
like stone
as the argument moved to weighing
the greater injustice:
to free a man who murdered another
or to punish a man who had done no wrong.

With anywhere as better than where
we were at
with doing anything else as better than
what we had to do
while the gravity of our call sunk us dismally
we weighed the truth in balances of justice.

How much of the evil we see in others
is actually our own?

As it is written, "He who calls
a man a fool is already guilty of murder.

Blizzard

Coming down
in swirls so thick,
the blizzard closes in
upon us all
until there is
only the thickness
of the snow
filling the entirety of space entirely
as the wind
scatters the flakes
in an immaculate devastation
and the heart hungers
in such desolation
that the burdened land
cries out through its cover
of snow –
yet, a lone gull
advances upon the sky
with somewhere to be.

What appears impossible is the work
of the invisible, that substance more
true than any person could grasp,
while Paul said: "For what is seen
is temporary, but what is unseen is eternal."

Darkness with its
razor edge moves
across the throat of this eve
of snow blown through the sky
as the cold crunches
beneath the tires
and I drive blind to all
except the oblivion
of this journey
that is timeless in its whip
of wind and white
encompassing me
with its silent sweep of death
holding my travel
in peril with a slip
to one side, then the other
as I grasp the steering wheel
thinking that life detaches itself
from loose ends of this nothingness
feeling the road fall
from its stretch to home
believing that inch by inch
ever so slowly I will arrive
safely in my nest –
yet, the freeze and the ice
is ever out there to maul me
with its lethal claws
while the lone gull rests.

To be captured and enslaved by the grip
of death
casts the heart into a vast wasteland,
but Paul says:
"Now the Lord is the Spirit, and where the Spirit
of the Lord is, there is freedom."

Dawn awakens the sky
to the light glistening
over snow capped fields frozen
while the crisp cold crackles
across the land wild with white
and wanting to sleep forever
but never able to sleep long enough
while the sun with lucid luster
touches the heavens and moves
the heart to beat
one day longer than it should
since the heavy hush
of wind bristles through bush bright
alive with the sparkle of dawn
that lifts its head that rises
full faced and beaming with a glow –
yet, the delicate drama
of this dance knows
no end as my heart
as an artifact articulates
onto the sky blue, as I drive ever on
and time itself sifts through
an ancient rhyme that speaks
uncertain curves about certain truths
in the way of the wind
beginning with omega
and leading to the alpha of us all
although again the lone seagull soars.

To be ever upon the brink
of being no more opens a truer vision
to what is – yet, Paul said:
Now we see but a poor reflection;
then we shall see face to face.
Now I know in part; then I shall know
fully, even as I am fully known.

This thing called Love

To be with my love
as the wind, gentle,
tumbles into deeper flames of azure,
deeper than a summer's eve –
to be forever upon the mountain
where hope is born
in the look
of her eyes, brighter
than a night's dawn –
to be within the forest
where her dance
depicts a verdant truth,
longer than a quiet day –
suddenly, a song escapes
into the air while she is there.

As it is written: "God so loved the world
that he gave his one and only son,
that whoever believes in him shall not
perish but have eternal life."

If it were not for the truth in the encompassing
of love there would only be nothingness in
itself echoing through the hollow chambers
of a mindless heart, but the truth of love lives,
so we move together beyond our own selves.

As the Christ hung on a cross with His mother
and the disciple whom He loved standing near,
He said: "Dear woman, here is your son,"
and to the disciple He said: "Here is your mother."

Softly but swiftly
is her step along the sway
of her way, as a chorus
of doves coos tenderly
about her form.

As the Christ hung on a cross
beaten by the wrath of God
because of what we had done
and what we had left undone,
He said: "Forgive them Lord,
for they know not what they do."

Nothingness ceases even as possibility
where love rubs truth into being more than
itself, and that is where one soul
touches another
as the moments ease their way into eternity.

As the Christ hung on a cross
as His pain disfigured His features,
He said: "I thirst."

Where does she go?
I do not ask
but only follow,
for she owns the stars
of an endless sky,
the swirling planets
and all of their mysteries
in substance and symmetry,
and she owns the very meat
of my heart beat.

As the Christ hung on a cross, He said
to one being crucified along side Him:
"I tell you the truth, today you will be
with me in paradise."

Because there is love, there always already
is being rather than nothingness, as we, together,
exist as the immanent transcendence
that belongs
to the soul, as that comprehensive actuality.

As the Christ hung on a cross, He said:
"My God, my God, why have you forsaken
me?"

In her breath she holds
a constellation
of violets, as I look
into the smile
upon her face,
her lips like liquid fire
seeping into the space
of my heart and rinsing
the fibers of my mind
with a solitary flame
of being there.

As the Christ hung on a cross,
a sacrifice to the Most High God
for our transgressions, He said:
"Father, into your hands I commit my spirit."

Dean C. Gardner

What look she has
is more of a secret treasure
to see, to feel,
to hold forever,
and what is there
is enough to erase
nothingness from all being.

As the Christ hung on a cross
to pay our debt to God, He said:
"It is accomplished."

What is this thing called love?

Being There

It is so hot,
while the warmest day
of the year
buckles
the streets,
while the birds
drop
from the trees
dried up and dead,
while the dog
pants
too exhausted
even in the shade
to wag its tail,
and the cloudless sky
seers
the earth
with all
that is there.

It is always something and never nothing,
for nothingness in itself is impossible, a pure
linguistic fiction, while as an absence it
can be grasped as a lack of everything.

As it is written, there is
"a time to search
and a time to give up searching."

Watermelon
fresh
from icy cold
and more than sweet
more than succulent
when each morsel
soothes
the tongue
with a taste
more pure
than joy itself
more true
than being there
when the mouth
awakens
to a perfect pleasure
of immeasurable delight,
and the mind
eases
from its space
caged
in a heat's sweat.

Being is always toward something
as defined by possibility and through
experiencing possibility, being affirms
itself by developing expectancy.

As it is written, there is
"a time to tear down
and a time to build."

It is
so cold,
the coldest day
of the year
with the long walk
from the stranded car
bitter, piercing
as the wind
tortures
the bones
with its
deep bite
while each step
through the snow
steals breath
from a frozen chest
and being there
brings one
that much closer
to the brutality
in what is there.

To believe is to know beyond the appearance
of a matter and into its substance, grasping
that which is the face behind all of the masks
as being moves itself into yet another form.

As it is written, there is
"a time to scatter stones
and a time to gather them."

The hot cocoa
is rich
and soothing
on the tongue
while it is
swished
around the mouth
while the cup
warms
the hands
while the scent
fills the air
with a delicious aroma –
yet it speaks
a subtle gentleness
known
to simple comforts
as if being there
not only mattered
but was enough
not only
for the moment
but for all times.

Reality is a mirror for self to assert its being,
while actuality is a window for self to behold
and to leap beyond all and everything
within as well as what is out there.

As it is written, there is
"a time to be silent
and a time to speak."

To visit the had been, the once upon a time,
not a fiction though, but a reconstructed mythology,
so perilous, if ensnared in what is no longer –
yet, if one does not know out of what
one has become what one is, can one plot
one's course to get to one's calling ? – or,
does one's calling call one's being from the myth
of one's self into the veritable substance
of the everlasting by the power of the Call.

The Flowers of Forever

At the very top of a blue spruce
swaying back and forth in gusts of wind
at the very top of what is ever known
a blue jay announces the end of the day
to the blue of a deeper blue sky –
yet, the blue of the spruce, the blue
of the jay and the blue of the evening sky
are all as truly blue as the blood of all
our veins is all truly red.

Although there is a truth to the sound
of the jay, although there is an essential
meaning released into the dusk of another day
by the jay clinging up high, although
the veritable secrets of all that exists
are carried through the cracks in the wind,
nothing is moved by his eloquent message.

Here,
the tragedy of our being is spelled out boldly.

It is not that everyone knows everything
or that everyone knows nothing;
it is not that anyone knows everything
or that no one knows something; for all know
better than to listen to what matters most.

The color of despair
is indeed deep, bitter and clamorous.

To the left are the jaws of the young lioness;
to the right are the horns of a rage-filled bull;
below are the fangs of treacherous vipers;
above circle hungry vultures, waiting, waiting;
thus is each day that is not unlike any other.

As it is written, "Even though I walk
through the valley of the shadow of death,
I will fear no evil, for you, Oh Lord, are with me;
your rod and your staff, they comfort me."

In fact, when seeing clearly, the blue
of the blue spruce, the blue of the blue jay,
the blue of the evening sky – are not truly blue,
none of them; for blue is imaginary as are
all things of this or any other world
just as blood is not red when it is overlooked.

To mourn for the times that never have been
to grieve for the joys that never were there
to stand upon the railing before the abyss
and leap into a new life where hope abounds –
how solemnly the bell tolls over the lost
as dust covers dreams and we return to dust –
yet, there is no turning back from tomorrow
when today only knows the ache to being.

Each tic of the clock drives deeper the stake
in the heart. Each drop of rain is another
fathom of despair drowning our dreams.

As it is written, "Come to me all
who are burdened and heavy laiden,
and I will give you rest."

When the darkness of this world
seeps into the heart, filling each corner
of its dwelling with debilitating disease
as the heart's rhythmic beat turns to a flutter
and then a final dull thud, as the blood
in the passage ways of the mind
dries and turns to dust and the nectar
that nourishes the spirit rots from abuse
this soul seeks that light of deliverance
looks for that breath of hope for life
and from its perch high above our pain
the blue jay vanishes into the night
taking with it, its message of infinite meaning.

However,
as we follow the advance of days
with the sun reaching through
        the eternal blue
as our steps find the footing of solid ground
and our minds rest upon a gentler earth
as our eyes light upon the arc
of a rainbow glittering in heavens of hope
there is a healing even for the deepest
wounds,
there is a blessing even for the poor in spirit
as the blue jay returns to the top
of the blue spruce amid patches of
a bluer blue
in a new dawn and the dirge of wind
it has ceased. A calm has found us.

It is that all blues are a blossoming in the mind
with all blood as one red bloom toward being
and we become the flowers of forever
growing out of the earth of the Lord's divine will.

When despair insists,
life persists.

As it is written, "Thank you Lord for
my affliction, so I may learn your statutes."

The Target

During rush hour
on the way to work,
before tenderly tapping
my bumper
the lady
through the rear-view mirror
pounded
her steering wheel
as traffic
packed tighter and tighter
from three lanes
to one.

Life as always too short and death
as forever
while patience used to be a virtue,
leads one
to wonder about the purpose
of the hurry,
as the clock in the chest grinds us down
to dust.

Already, the heat
from the pavement,
the fumes
from the engines,
the crawl
of the cars,
buses, trucks and rigs
went on and on
as two clouds,
so very white,
played across an otherwise
blue hovering, seeing sky.

postModerns are forever going somewhere
with seldom truly being anywhere, as human
tragedy becomes a way of life, a whining
trajectory of a formless force targeting
everyone.

The frisking about
and comic acrobatics
within the broil of blue
of these two dainty dabs
in white
circused their bodies
for all the world to see
as they out-witted
any king's tumblers
with their free-form flow,
and an eye
hanging onto them
found a romp and frolic –
reprieve
from the stack
of wheels
harnessed to the road,
as the lady
from behind squeezed
in front of me,
yet I eased back
to give her space.

Curious: how even death does not give
a proper perspective to life, as what we believe
distances from what we are, which distances
from what we do - as if it did not matter?

Although some gluttons
of gore grazed
on the carnage,
the grizzly bits
of bent and twisted life spent
and dripping onto the concrete,
I did not
entertain a moment
with the explosion
of that daylight scene –
better not to gawk
at others' misfortune –
the tragedy avoidable
by one good look back,
but I drove onward
to a day of work
to earn a little liberty
for my family.

It seems as though eventually at
some point,
justice is an invisible force following
each of us
until that very moment when all
of the truly good
we so duly deserve finally takes us
by the throat.

Not much later
driving down the pike,
the clot
in traffic passed,
I scanned the sky
for those two clouds
but found
that they had disappeared,
as the lady,
who pounded her steering wheel,
who snuggled
my rear bumper,
who squeezed her way
in and out of traffic,
was pulled over
with a scream
of flashing lights –
she wishing
her citation
would also disappear.

As the teacher said:
"Meaningless. Meaningless.
Everything is meaningless."

The Crow

In a land of snow
where the wind blows cold
and the knuckles and knees feel how
unforgiving winter is,
the crow attaches himself
to a pine bough
waiting for a harvest
of snowflakes to launch the day
with the breath of the everlasting,
and he listens with head cocked
to the groaning of time
that which has no form but has substance
that holds no shape but lives in truth
as the dawn throbs its color
again into fragile mortality
as the light escapes from the edges
of a world that thinks into being there.

To those who cling to the note
of the authentic, to those who forget
that they will be forgotten, to those
who on jagged shards stretch
a look into what they truly are,
what is this thing called a crow?

The blackness of this crow
a pitch deeper than a sky filled with night,
knows the music of immortality,
remembering that he is only in the mind,
and it is his blackness
that confesses the wants of the day,
the haunts of being too little
too much of the time, as the snow
answers in white with ruts of gray
as the sky passes silent in its way
and the sun reaches into the eyes
taking the part of blackness
that belongs to the blood of the crow –
yet, to all this there is a calm
as if on swift feet time ran away
leaving only prints in the snow
where the gathering of the cold followed.

It is that the call
of the crow suffers
across white fields laid
with the bitter bite of cold
as the sun motions the air
with a harsher light
as the clouds drop their gray
in a formless reaching of the heart
where no warmth eases the stay –
yet it is the call of the crow
to be there, strategic in his stand
as if meaning something more
than the weight of its rasping tone
that voice drunk on the wilds
and the crow's call moves
the soul to know the cut of the truth.

Noble crow, on wings of black velvet
you rise from your silhouette
as you circle the air with a look
to the white of the land,
but what dream do you glean
from your vision from above,
where do you part from life,
and how do you serve the Christ?

Disappearing into the daylight
erased from being what he is
the crow leaves only a trace that dangles
in the awe of the moment
for it is that he is ever so long gone
that the wind is a rampage of chills
and that the snow is forever there
as time stutters a vacant syllable
of being awake to his absence,
that act of a will done in black
punctuated in the blank page
of mind spinning in frigid gusts –
yet in the heart of questions
only the crow is an answer
in a white world beneath a shroud
of clouds
when the blood of being
drops tears across the hills
as the archetype of the now
shows through the white, white snow
and the only reason for the crow
is to call to question the nature of form.

As what stirs the spirit toward the heart
of being, as what is there is the stone
of substance, as what matters most occurs
between the dancing of a solitary snowflake
to the dirge of another dreary dawn
and the nodding of a withered weed, the echo
of his call fashions an eerie wonder
since God created the physics
of the crow and the cold.

A Man's Life

In a night
of a stillness
with the quiet
of the dark
and the glitter
of the heavens,
as the city slept
dreaming in peace
and comforted by rest
at last,
with the roads clear
of a honk and beep,
a man
searched
for someone . . .
something.

What value has every human life as billions
swarm nameless around and about, here
and there, and when do we reach even
to someone, if not until finally it is too late?

As dawn approached
a man alone
in his life
sought,
but no ear listened
to his cries, his plea
falling empty
no gate
opened
to his wreckage,
no kindness
from anywhere
resonated
within his soul,
so he sought
all the more
in that quiet
before the dawn,
void and desperate
in his void.

The world gnaws the bones of each of us
while the pains of being too little in too much
can grab the spirit of even the strongest soul
and snap it, devour it, leaving it as
so much waste.

He must have
looked everywhere
for some compassion,
some touch of love,
but he did not
turn to God
with his bleeding need.

When in pain, every man is alone in pain
as the fluid of even a remote hope
keeps the heart from attacking the mind, until
even that becomes a knot around the throat.

As the sun rose
its warmth gentle,
its light radiant,
as the dew
on the lawn twinkled
like stars
on the green,
as the blossoms
unfolded
with their quiet grandeur,
as all the city greeted
the freshness
of a new day –
a man hanged himself
by his shoelaces
in a boulevard tree.

Attending to their duty,
the officials
roped off the area,
cut him down,
and readied the street
for a new day's traffic,
the street looking
as good as new.

Curious: even after death, life goes on,
as the glow from pockets of kindness
fills the no longer with more than reason
to continue this journey down to its end.

Dean C. Gardner

Long afterward,
cuddled in the warmth
of a winter's bed,
the covers
pulled over
and the wife
snuggled near,
we watched
the drama
unfold
on television
of a nameless man
hanging from a tree
by his shoelaces.

How cheap –
a man's life.

What treasure –
someone who cares . . .

As it is written:
"In his own image,
God made man."

Garden

Let us go gently
into the garden,
watch the light
on the pond
reflect through our mind
reflecting on the light,
the pond, the garden,
drifting slowly
through a still space
an avenue of song
lifted to the sky;
then to feel the glimmer
that supple sparkle
of a hope
drawn near and embraced,
those sweet scents
of blossoms
rich with delight
lofting through the air
as the garden
it blooms,
as the breeze
it whispers
as delicate
the light dances silently
in radiant splendor.

To linger there longer with rest for the mind
where true light bathes the pilgrim tenderly
as a bouquet of warm wraps the soul
in a glow –
where is this garden of solace for the weary?

God
touched this place
with peace
as the little green frog
nudges
near the edge
of the pool
cool and clear
as the lily's white
flowers
with immaculate grace,
and the reeds sway
as a distant melody
of a red wing blackbird
eases
through the ferns
lush in their green
yet quiet
in their majesty.

Is there such a place where what
is within
reach is all the invisible veritable truth,
a treasure
of pleasurable dreams and revitalized,
nobler joys
as a yearning of the human condition
made visible?

As an old
mud turtle
pokes its head
along side
a lily pad,
here,
cradled in the garden
there is only life
as the breath
of peace passes
through the air
a deep waft
of a deeper feel,
an overture woven
through the fabric
of the music of being
being full, rich and abundant,
as tiny ripples
follow the turtle's head
to the far reaches
of the very end of the pond,
and the little brown duck
smiles serenely
while knee deep
in the shallows
on this side.

Impossible! Could there ever be
such a space
floating around and about as
a common glory
forever deep and ever so steadily
and fluidly flowing
as if it is a kingdom come
of peace everlasting?

Dean C. Gardner

As the sun sets
and the sky is aglow,
as the little brown duck
nestles its down
and the old turtle
snuggles
in the deep,
the crickets rise
to serenade
the moon
swaying slowly
in the heavens
while fireflies dance
with merriment.

Certainly, that somewhere is a place
not of this
world, where peace and joy, as a song
in a garden,
harmonize together as if a purer dream
yet truer,
a reborn breath where in the heart
is our God.

That Winter Night

Another night
mother
was out late again
with her own
life style to support,
and Dad
had been gone
to somewhere
for longer
than their memory could serve
as three
little latch-key kids
nestled in quiet,
the winter winds pounding
outside.

It is that irresponsibility is an
unlearned behavior
as parents unlearn to care for
their children
and children accept neglect as a way
of life
that they are there but for no
true purpose.

Dean C. Gardner

Midnight
and all through the house
cold struck
from all corners
as the furnace
went out again,
as the three children
awoke,
a chill through their bones
and the eldest
of the three,
then nine years,
turned on the space heater
to get some warmth
as mother
danced
the night alive
as father
was forever absent
a faceless name.

Even when quite young, children often
know what needs to be done
and are capable
of at times of the extraordinary
depending upon what precisely
is the occasion.

As the room
grew warm
the three little children
snuggled together
before the space heater
with the cold winter wind
a din out there
in the night –
yet they fell asleep
in each other's arms
beneath blankets
of heat
and they dreamed
of a time
when they would be
a family
with a real mother and father
and all bundled together
with an enduring care.

Sweet dreams are true only as dreams
for what is there at times does not change
but they are good as a source of hope
for without hope there is only what is there.

At 2:12 a.m.
the eldest awoke
to a room
filled with flames,
grabbed the two others
and found
a way out
to the bitter cold
winter night
as mother drank her nightcap
in a nearby bar –
oblivious
to the inferno,
oblivious
to her children
in the cold winter night,
their home in flames.

A little later
amid the crowd and sirens –
"My babies,"
blubbered the mother
"What have you done?"

"Mommy" the eldest
cried,
"Where have you been?"

Fortunately,
the three children survived
for another day.

Unfortunately,
the older couple
on the second floor
apartment
in that house –
oblivious in their sleep –
was consumed
by the blaze
that winter night.

Dean C. Gardner

As a Word: Suspension

The shadows
of the leaves
and the leaves
themselves –
no less near
than the word
"leaves"
and the leaves
themselves.

How the movement
of the moment
of their play
through sunlight
upon the window
takes what he is
and carries it
away already.

Between
quickened breaths,
he floats
in the shade
as who he is
disconnects
from any
and all space
and he becomes
the rub
of distance
beyond time.

The shade
belongs
to no dimension
although the leaves
of light
cascade across the shadows
and both are there
as he hovers
his mind
somewhere
between this and that,
feeling the power
of some hand
holding his soul.

With no light there would be no leaves,
there would be no shade from the leaves,
and he would unfold as a center
of another void.

With no source of meaning there
would be no
words and he would be a tangent
of nothingness:
belief – that trace to true meaning,
Jehovah God.

Encrypted
in the silence
of the shade,
death writes,
"The sacrifice
of Christ
and then His
resurrection –
so we may live
forevermore."

The Pulse of a Meaning

Quiet,
the night
in a tendril's grasp
and that
of a heart's
caressed love –
it is the music
of the garden
growing glorious,
blooming
as the moon
glows
in the starlit night
as a solitary drop
of dew clings
to the breath
of a wind
through reeds
and weeds
of darkness
fitted tight.

The garden means many things but mostly
it means
when it is not; for when filled with song
the shower
of the soul in the garden shows itself,
but when
the song is gone, it conceals itself
in the always.

What the lover
knows
as the bloom true
and what the night
holds
in a silent stir,
the garden
opens
as the pulse
of a meaning
passing
through the grace
of each blossom
known
as a whisper
told
to the wind
shown
as the light
cascading
from a thin slice
of moon.

With never a before and never an after,
in the garden it is always already forever
as time is liberated by giving
a heart's space
to the Immaculate Incarnate Word behind
all eternity.

Quivering
as if a longing
of fathoms
beneath the deep,
the lilies
speak their soft scents
into the lovely,
a melodious murmuring
of mind
through a kindlier matter,
a yearning throb
yet a quickened pulse
as if an awakening
brewing inside
an opulent pot
of souls and angels,
while stars
drop their glitter
upon verdant breaths
a passage
more of promise
than passion,
more a hand
of gentle gestures
as darkness
in the blooms
grows still.

What truth is held in some shards
of words,
the blooms never say, except
those born
of an eternal moment beyond a seeing
of celestial splendor, upon
a stroll of star petals.

Dean C. Gardner

The garden
at the ease
of night,
always of lovers
lingering by,
becomes that interlude
in the everlasting,
as visions
leap over
and beyond horizons
known
and the flowers
bow nobly
their delicate crowns
before the stars
and moon
with our souls there
forever.

Internment

While the grasses groaned slowly green
and the tulips raised their voices in praise
with a chorus of crocuses in the gentle
and warm
swaying before the face of the sun hung
over the budding bones of limbs and boughs,
while an agile nook of shadow and a fragile
mind met in an awakening, that rhyme
of breath
born on wings and downy things that coo
and tweet, chirp and sing, while the glow
of spring soared through the air, he dared
to wonder whether this was his last season,
his last day, as if the parade of todays
should cease, as if the grave in the wide skies
was to be his home throughout all eternity
and whether tomorrows would only be
a dream.

Looking into his hands, the creases
of years passing him away, the calluses
of time
wearing into his fingers, the age spots
marking his moments like tombstones,
he wondered how he became who he was
as a cloud frolicked by destined to vanish
before it got anywhere and the nymph
of spring
that capricious curl of succulent green twirled
its magic wand, unfurled its verdant cloak
and laid to rest winter's wild tirade of cold
as if that mattered more than all his years.

It was that he grew cold in his bones
despite the warming air, the green spring rain,
the smell of the earth awakening from its
primordial pit with that subtle speech
of the new
born land, but it was that he lived enough
to know that he had lived enough to know better
than to believe in the mist of the spring air
the fog thick and clinging to the hollows
and trees or the sun that seemed to be forever
rising as a morning in March chose him to see
the passage of his stay through the seasons
as he wondered why this spring and he
were there.

All the years, those treasures of an aging man
condemned by a warming
in a budded bough –
a cruel play of time.

There grew in his heart a stillness
but not a calm, a silence but not a quiet
a rest but not a peace, as a tightrope
snapped
between a lazy spring day and being there
which became the grip knotting his brow
the tweak twitching his flanks, the lump
clotting his brain as a robin tugged
on a fat worm with the cat eyeing, the dog
pointing, the earth sighing and the sky
that haven of the hereafter, covering over
and he wondered when his time would expire
what he could do to make things right
and how he could endure to his last breath.

Bent by a broken spirit, he dropped
to his knees, bowed his head and wept,
his arthritic hands holding a countenance of tears
with a trembling through his limbs that bludgeoned
and drained his heart until he faded
into his own shadow, as what mattered most
to him he knew did not truly matter,
as the vacuity of his days consumed him
into being a feeble remnant decaying
in the dust,
a tattered rag worn out by meaninglessness,
his life as a passage of nothingness
into the void.

In a wild, wired and raging sea
the ebb of being
looks up.

From the deep within his insides, gently,
a voice whispered, more of a moving sound
like a rush of wind through the back
of the mind
than a distinguishable word, more of a feeling
that brought breath to his heart, and it raised
his face with a hopeful hue as he said,
"Dear Jesus, is that you?" It was that Christ
spoke to his heart, pulling him from the grave
that was his dwelling, the tomb that was his
living for all his life. It was that the Jesus
he sang to
in his youth came to him in his need
seeing beyond his fault, and giving him
the breath of hope as the sun shone down
from the heavens he knew was home. It was
spring awakening in his heart as he leaped
out of himself, embracing the joy that only
comes from being right with God, and raising
his hands he said, "Thank you Lord for being
the way, the truth and the life."

Being caught in the web of darkness:
the lamp of the living Christ –
freedom and hope.

Although the divide between the tic of spring
and the cavity of his despair
multiplied distance
between his heart, purpose and the call
of the greening bough, although the meaning
within his grip dropped through a spent mind
as his affliction tightened
his brow,
he was found by a whisper reverberating
within his soul, the trace of an echo
from his far away youth, as Christ lived
all the while waiting for him to awaken
to the peace that passes all understanding.

Within the trappings of being
to the beyond, within Christ triumphs –
a celebration of the soul.

Dean C. Gardner

The Language of Love

Lovely she
perched
in exotic beauty
and her air
perfumes his universe.

When love is green as a meadow in spring
is that welcomed green and the appetite
of the heart
is greater than the eye, all and everything
rushes
at once in a race to an uncertain place.

Ever so quietly
the earth
grows closer
ever closer
between them.

Lifted heavenward, her face in the clouds
those eyes that hold celestial promise
that chin carved from a curious cumulus
wages war on the soft parts of the mind
until the image removed from all thought
basks in an infusion of light as if knowing
the place where love was meant to be
while in the high parts of the sky lingers
a pocket of rockets destined to explode
the quiet of the moon, and it means to pull
the trigger on nothingness as the wind
waves in wonder and delight, as yesterday
leaps over the walls of decades.

See her eyes lit with stars, her lips
kissed with blossoms of a deeper blood
than the rose, and hear her voice of a wind
through a garden of growing joys.

Feel her walk with a sway to the hip
as her scent carries your heart
over the beams of a crescent moon
as the night fills the sky with star breaths.

Dean C. Gardner

Silence
between them
a look
a stir
and the thunder
of ages past
of women and their men
of men and their women
the thunder
of loves past –
gawk
at this man
and this woman –
gawk
in awe
in silence
before these two souls
entwined
in an eternal embrace.

It is that love is as it is
the sound of the thrush before morning
the tickle in the taste of a sunrise
or the shoot of a cloud in the encompassing,
and it is that love never was as it is
the breath departing from a broken wind
the thick of a heart in a wild moon
or the root of a cloud through the beyond.

While the better breaths of life were meant
to be cherished, while all of love
is meant to be lived, it plays a melody
beyond youth, although it resounds
in your heart; although youth can shuffle
its feet, it knows not how to dance
the enduring dance; although it can hum along,
youth knows not the language of the music of love.

She is the movement
of stars
the movement
of their planets
the movement
of a fertile crescent
of moon
and angels
write their name
on each other's heart
with stardust.

To gather from the garden of love
is to be filled with the blooms of sacrifice
leaping out of the self and embracing
the other,
enduring because of the good, through the sad
and the indifferent, through the trials and pain
until the chosen fruit of love chooses to ripen
as the blossom is never more precious
than the fruit.

Although the tender touch of a beloved's breath
wets the neck with a quiver and a sigh,
although the look in the eyes dreams dreams
finer than the last frost of spring,
do not confuse the pleasures of romance
with the service of love. Romance is fleeting
while love has stamina. Romance is fed
by passion,
while love is fed by devotion. Romance
is a trinket while love is a jewel.
Romance may lead to love
while true love always leads to God.
A youthful heart was made for romance
while love was meant forever.

Dean C. Gardner

So drink deeply from the cup of passion,
savor its succulent brew with ravenous awe
until you glow as the moon and the stars
fill your heart with its liquid fire
until you melt into a senseless pool of vapors
and as you stagger, wild-eyed, delirious
remember always that it may lead to love.

Learn the beat of her feet
along her chosen path, the rhythm
of her heart, the song of her mind
and run with her through the streets of heaven.

Teach her to ache for the truth
as the very substance of her being
and to grow out of the timeless void
into a warm and gentle breath.

Give her the star that dwells in your heart
share with her the children of the light
and know that one day your tomorrows
will quietly step into the glow of love.

How humble
a man before beauty
how humble
before the grandeur
and grace of beauty
how humble
Adam
must have been
with first sight
of his Eve.

Such blessing
beauty
forever is.
As it is written, "And now these three remain:
faith, hope and love. But the greatest of these
is love."

Fairy Tale

There once was
a young family,
a father and mother
and an only daughter,
as times were lean
and pennies were counted
as hard decisions
cut between convenience
necessity and sacrifice
with extravagance not
a consideration,
while what mattered
most was service
to the Lord.

As it says in Scripture:
"What good is it, my brothers,
if a man claims to have faith
but has no deeds?"

For all that we do
let it not be done
from a spirit burdened
by blind obedience
or duty or out of guilt –
for such motivators
are legalistic, breed bitterness
and sever the soul.

A good Friday passed
led to a Saturday
and the mother suggested
to her husband
that he take
their daughter
to a matinee
while the wife did domestic chores –
such an experience
the daughter never had before.

As it says in Scripture:
"Who is wise and understanding
among you? Let him show it
by his good life, by deeds done
in the humility that comes from wisdom."

All sons are special sons
and equally are all daughters special
for this time, for all time, forever.

The young father
beckoned the daughter
to come to him
and she did; then,
he told her
their Saturday plan.

As it says in Scripture:
"What is your life? You
are a mist that appears for a little
while and then vanishes."

To not grasp the difference
between sacrifice, necessity, convenience
and extravagance is to rape the hearts
of those who love you; for those who love
you are the measure of the difference.

The only daughter
leapt
upon her daddy's lap
giving him hugs
giving him kisses;
then, with a light bright
in her eyes
that sparkled with love
she jumped
to the floor
and began to pick up all
of her toys
to put them away
in her treasure chest
in her room.

As it says in Scripture:
"But the fruit of the Spirit is love,
joy, peace, patience, kindness, goodness,
faithfulness, gentleness and self-control.
Against such things there is no law."

For all that we do
let it be done
because of thankfulness
to the Almighty –
with such a source, the endeavor
is a fruit of the Spirit
and a gift from God.

After all, justification
by faith in Christ Jesus precedes;
then, good works follow
through the light
of the Holy Spirit.

And that is why
the only daughter picked up
her mess without being told
to do so.

Dean C. Gardner

Dirt Bike Racers
. . . for Elders Dillon & Clausing

As the sun
baked the heat hot,
as rubber beat the dirt round
as the men of mean thunder
red-lined through the dust
all and everyone sniffed the wind
and time wound up.

It was that the race
went to the swift
with lightning bleeding
through their veins
as these men
of mean thunder
cut quickness into the scene.

All of life is forevermore
a victory pass through the grit
while nothing means more
than somehow pulling through.

There was less
of the roar in the wind
and more of the butterflies
bantering their havoc . . .
for some;
then, only the idle
of the dirt oval,
the quiet before the quick.

Three of the riders,
Kainz on 51, Thompson on 62
and Cortazzo on 5
sat tall enough at the line
measured by the intensity
in the whites of their stares
and they rolled down
the path to combat
steel tempered in the sun.

All of life
is one long spring dream
as the summer spoke itself
before watchful eyes,
but time treasured
one more pass
through the eye of the needle.

Courage never knows evil
but the truth beyond oneself,
only, as this was life
and that was death
while winning pushed the soul
into being.

Dean C. Gardner

Cutthroat hung back in stealth
while the burning tires wailed
through the gauntlet,
the air thick with the drift
of rubber
and the day was put to rest.

While the metal of men
was measured by the handshake
of courage and faith,
the first of the one-armed racers
took a victory lap
in the soul of humankind
and the heart of God.

"May the Lord bless you
and keep you; may the Lord
make his face to shine upon you,
and may he be gracious
unto you, and give you peace."

A Calling

Stone against stone
bone against bone
that is the way it is
as the bodies
of celestial dynasties
rub being there into being.

Steel against steel
wheel against wheel
that is the way it is.

He looked down
upon a darkness
where figures shone as gold
upon a path of light
as they walked
with messages in their heart.

He did not know
why he was placed on high
or why they were set low;
that was the way it was.

The scene, itself
was a message
the wealth of its insight
beyond his reach
teaching him what was right
through a vision of symbols, of signs
but the meaning of the view
the direction of its point
a correction for his life, he was certain
seemed beyond his reach
so he drew thoughts
from the good that was there
so he meditated upon passages
so he waited.

Time moved its fingers
across grooves of prayerful thought
some eluding his catch
some that he caught
and he knew
that what he sought
was the way to grow his life
as he grew toward an understanding
of what he must do.

To flee
the grip of evil
is good.

To control and enslave
through the manipulation of powers
is evil.

To serve
with a clean heart
is a gift.

From on high
held by a cloud, pure and white
was an iron tongs
and in its jaws
an ember burned.

As the cloud approached him
his seeing grew large
and it touched his lips
with the ember, searing hot.

There was no pain
only relief.

Ten thousand, thousand angels
came toward him then;
they were his army
for the war of the end times.

Stone against stone
bone against bone
that is the way it is
as the bodies
of celestial dynasties
rub being there into being.

Steel against steel
wheel against wheel
that is the way it is.

As it is written,
"Here am I Lord.
Send me. Send me."

Sensibilities of Being

To know
experiential by kind
accepts what is there
because it appeals
to the five senses
because it is of the veritable;
it exists as a known
conforming to the regiment
of being in time and space.

The table is there
as one sees it, feels it
the table revealing
what it is
by one seeing it, feeling it
and conforming to the idea
of what constitutes
a table.

To know
gathers what is there
from what is external
to the self as a given.

Dean C. Gardner

To think
a processing of form and substance
conforms to the mechanism
of a kind of logic
a type of reasoning
taking what is there
whether internal or external
and seeking
both similarity and difference
between the subject
of the thinking
and the domain of the known.

To think
positions what is there
as a known
as a means of making something
into a given
by acquainting the self
with what a thing is
and what a thing is not;
it is of the virtual.

A thought is
as it is employed
the employing
defining what constitutes
a thought.

To imagine
departs from the given
from the domain
of knowing
and leaves the comforts
of thinking, of reason
and regular kinds of logic
behind.

There are no rules
to imagining
no regulators that govern
the ways to imagine.

It is neither a proof
or a proving
but rather a probing
and a leaping
outside the limitations and boundaries
of the given and of thinking.

Imagining occurs
by an excitation
of the ideas behind the given
by the ungrounding
of processing form and substance.

The domain
of imagining
is endless possibility.

Dean C. Gardner

To believe
is to be called upon
by the unknown
a speaking to the in-most self
an endearment
by that which is not
of the given, is trustworthy and primordial
and conforms to its own kind of mechanism
its own reason.

Its form and substance
cannot be manipulated
by thought
but it purposes into motion
a sympathetic resonance
within the self.

To believe
is the calling of the unknown
a calling
that empowers the self
to choose to do good
or to yield to an authority
which controls what the self does.

The self
either accepts the believing
or chooses unbelief.

So there are
four sensibilities of being:
knowing, thinking, imagining
and believing.

Each
has a place
in the growth of a life.

As it is written,
"Trust in the Lord with all your heart
and lean not on your own understanding."

Dean C. Gardner

Special Knowledge

A man looks
and what he sees
is there before him
as a cooling breeze
stirs his thoughts
to envision
the invasion of truth
onto the scene.
So he looks
upon a wall of brick and mortar
sturdy, solid, thick
and he sees the wall
for what it is
going no further
probing no further.

So another man
upon seeing the brick wall
parts the way
of his look
envisioning what his curiosity
his suspicions seek
his appetite hungering
for an insight, for special knowledge.

Is it a crime
to read between the lines?

Is it indecent
to want to know the truth?

Perhaps it simply is
that each has certain sensitivities
that someone's thinking
sets in motion
some certain sympathetic vibrations
and someone else tunes in on them
so it conforms to a law of physics.

But an accidental encounter
is not an invitation to visit
the bedroom of the mind.
So there is
a reason for walls.

So there is
a reason for a curtain
in the temple.

So is everything
merely an illusion
a myriad of veils
and to part one veil
to see what is there
is nothing more
than ascending in virtual reality.

But the code
of veritable reality
is a domain of stone-struck laws
made by the concrete of what is there
immutable.

There is an up.

There is a down.

There is what is
and there is what is right;
also, there is all that is not right.

So virtual reality
has a changing to it
that is constant;
it is whatever it is wanted to be.

The wind, calm
speaks with a rhythm, a rhyme
as a sweet balm
releases visions
that chime
with the special knowledge
of what is there
a ring gathered in diamond tones.

Puffs of wind
ruffle the scent
into a reaching
of the deep touch
until the drift
of what is there
lifts what is meant
into a gentle steeping
keeping clear the hutch
that is home to it.

A shadow traced
the length and breadth of it
the mystery of what was there
the special knowledge
revealed by a curiosity, a suspicion
uncovered by reading
the lips of the mind
motioning the calm
into an explosive commotion
of thoughts.

So, the sound
of the chimes
trickles down into fainting echoes
and even the least of them
grounds what is there
into the bedroom of the brain.

Dean C. Gardner

Still the body,
silent the lips,
until the wind tickles
from a curiosity, a suspicion
into an explosion
of generous giving
into an eruption
of mystery
that grooms the sky
of home and all its rooms.

Is it wrong
to do right?

Does up
come from under?

Perhaps it is not right
to uncover what is there
because of nothing more
than curiosity, suspicion.

Perhaps
what is covered
by the veils
is better left to rest there
and not be spirited into life.

To use what is not good
to unearth good
to manipulate the drift
of the wind
to read the lips of the mind
undresses the dignity
of what matters most.

To conjure up good
with evil incantations
is an abomination, a vile self-deception.

As it is written,
"I will cut off witchcraft out of your hand."
and "there shall not be among you a witch."

An Echo, Only

To think
into time and space
the splitting of when and where
as a train
rumbles through the distance
registering the moment
as an interval unfolding
leads one
to look beyond the darkness
beyond the here and now
into the light
that rubs the soul
into being.

The darkness
is the encompassing.

The stars
fight back the deep indigo sky.

The trees
are still in their stand.

When another train
howls in the night
an eerie pronouncement
of the important commerce
known to man's endeavor
the significance
of someone, anyone
becomes a lost art
an echo
that has faded
into the far side of oblivion.

What the eye sees
is darkness everywhere.

What the soul sees
is the hope in forevermore.

All of time
runs into the spaces
of darkness
a consuming blaze
of destruction
only to reveal
the rise of the soul
through the talk
of starlight
across the heavens
the sprinkling of hope
that brings life
through the perils
of being there.

So darkness
consumes life.

So darkness
voids being.

It is the longing of the soul
for what matters most
that launches
being into being there
with no constraint
of space
as when and where
are lifted above
the here and now
onto the horizon
that feeds the soul
with forevermore.

To be there
is to be beyond
time and space.

To be
is the trace
onto forevermore.

As it is written,
"For now we see in a mirror
dimly but then face to face;
now I know in part, but then
I shall know fully
just as I also have been fully known."

The Book of Books

Upon a dusty shelf
a dusty book cries out
to be read
its pages dripping
with two hundred years
of human wisdom.

Selections
from the Eighteenth and Nineteenth Century
document the thoughts
and the thinking
of great minds
that present their substance
to an age such as this.

The Age of Enlightenment
and that of Romanticism
are alive in the lives
of the now
but what is a man
left to his own devices
unless merely one more step
across a bridge
that spans the horizon
between the definite here
and the amorphous somewhere.

Dean C. Gardner

The workings of man's mind
the ideas it fastens to
in the long drift
of a long, long time
clear the clouds
from a dark, dark sky.

What is reason
if it is in love
with itself?

What is individualism
if it leads
only to despair?

Through the acrobatics
of language
man leaps from shadow
to more shadows
only to leave himself behind
a vast darkness
but there is a truth
before the wisdom of man
a sprinkling of light
across the ages.

The hungering words
of times past
and the thirsting words
of a time such as this
call upon the human heart
to seek an understanding
beyond itself
to gather the light
that points to a greater truth.
It is the Living Truth
in an open book
a book of books
upon the night stand
that knows the weight
of thoughtful thoughts
finding within its pages
the sweet message of deliverance
a passageway onto pure wonder.

How the Living Word
feeds the veritable
into the soul.

How this Book
opens the soul
to see the mind of Grace.

As it is written,
"All Scripture is given by inspiration of God
and is profitable . . ."

Dean C. Gardner

Bones

Since the hot heat of a summer's sun
melts the mind into a thick pool of oblivion
the dry bones of being there cry out for deliverance
but where in this broil is a hand of hope?

The sands
of the soul
pass through an hour glass
as time settles
in the sweat
of yet another hot day
the tyrannical sun
baking the life
out of being there.

There is
no breath
to the wind.

There is
no escape
from the encompassing inferno.

Alone
in the shade
of a lone tree
reveals the glare
of the day's blaze
an immutable noose
closing in on the throat
as time escapes
the grasp of the moment
as the dry rasping voice
of the soul
voids itself into a vast vacuum
of life.

How futile
the dream
of breath.

How senseless
being rubbed out
of life.
When the summer sun burns a hole in the soul
when it immobilizes muscle, as the lungs fill with parched earth
it is the dry bones of being there, crying out for mercy
that stirs the heart to hope onto living waters.

At dusk
the closeness of the thick air
thick with the broil
of a long, long, hot day
closes in around the mind
as thoughts droop
in a turmoil of sweat
destitute in their own sweat.

Dean C. Gardner

There is
no life
to these scorched bones.

Despair
is losing
the want of life.

But as it is written,
"Thus says the Lord God to these bones –
'Behold, I will cause breath to enter you
that you may come to life.'"

A Couple

Their voices
are like chimes
the chimes of eternity
the sound trailing off
into echoes
in body memory.

A perfume
fills the morning air
with a transfusion
of life giving life.

They are the song
growing the mountains
into the sky.

Their walk
along the sway of things
gathers a wonder
as the birds
gather around their feet
as a gentle breeze
warms the while
and a sun
full of roundness rises.

In the afternoon
at a café
they become the earth
of each other's life
exchanging worlds that flow
as the river of white clouds flows
and the sea of their selves
an indigo sea
deeper than pure ebony
bares a light onto forevermore.

They are
a family of one heart:
their look across the skies
fathomless.

The golden complexion
of their drift
where time extends through times
gathers a simple joy
that lingers, and lingers longer.

As they share what is there
their souls dance
from meadow to mountain.

The forests gather promise
for them
onto forevermore.

To take
what is not given
is a theft
and no good thing
can come of it.

To give
what is not takes
is the deception
of rejection.

To share
in the giving
takes one long, long time.

Where time and space
converge
into years and years and years
into decade after decades
they grow into an anthem
that celebrates
what true love
is all about.

How the gift
of being together
was a seed well planted.

After dinner
during quiet time
the sun sets unnoticed
as the talk leads
to children and grandchildren
and they lean on each other
much as they always had
a testament
through good times
and bad.

Dean C. Gardner

As the times changed
they followed one another
until time
all but left them behind
together.

As it is written,
"Cling to the bride of your youth."

Sought

To pull a thought
from the other side
of time and space
as ideas climb
out of their selves
to drift with celestial clouds
the ethereal fingers that trace
what is brought
upon the shelves
behind the mind
determines the destiny
of form, of structure
as what is born through substance
accrues a meaning of its own
a teaming of scenes and dreams
walking into sight.

It all confesses
that it is nothing more
than a procession of processes
walking into sight
through an opened door.

Dean C. Gardner

The breeze lifts gently
thought across the mind
upon wings that carry time, momentarily
that seize the firmament
indwelling its content
with the clouds, celestial by design
drifting contentedly, their signature
signed in the eyes of seeing.

It is not
the compass of the will
owned by any man
but the grand tale
of what is before a man
in power, strength, grace
that composes the bones of being
into the eyes of seeing.

Truth emits
a singular radiance, splendor
and to live its life
commits the soul
onto forevermore
along the way
where the truth says
in forms filled with substance
that times are ready
for harvest.

An immense silence
then erupts
from the jaws
gnawing time into dust
thrusting substance
into the ideas
of being there
where form chases a thought
pulled from the other side.

In what is there
nothing can hide.

So, to it
there is a singular truth
a drama of characters
seen among the unseen
characters visible
collected in the coliseum
of the eye
containing what is there
in the form of time's space
upon the balcony of mind.

Where does it go?

From where has it come?

The other side
wills being into being there
or so it thinks
as the silence disappears
into a rhythm
drawing time into the space
of being there.

Dean C. Gardner

So truth
is pulled from the other side
and the characters
that look on
see the unseen
the face of forevermore
the masks of being and time
upon a space
that defines itself
with colors that cannot be found
that sound like the groaning
from an alien ground.

To look into darkness
for true light
answers the question
before it is asked.

To look from darkness
for true light
asks for an answer
after questioning itself.

Truth
so lovely, so pure
emancipates being
from what is there
as prayerful thought sifts clarity
from celestial clouds
as time drifts truth
into substance, into form.

As it is written,
"Seek and you shall find.
Knock and it shall be opened onto you."

Monsters About

Turning his back
on the rising sun
he walked alone
through the darkness
the expanse
wrestling with his soul.

It was
that monsters of the expanse
were no less terrifying
than those
of the darkness within.

On both sides
were fearsome creatures
forces tearing apart
what a man is
a man of blood, bone and flesh
a man of thought and belief
and into the fiery jaws
of both sides he walked
ready to do battle
with all that was there
in the darkness.

There is a beautiful monster
her look a voluptuous form
and a man fills with desire
as she rubs his want
with her words and numbers
as her hair tangles with the moon
but as she rests a kiss
on her sweet muscles lips
she consumes all his breath
his lungs collapsed of body
his mind blighted with maggots
his life left a rotting carcass.

A man's desire
for a beauty
a devouring beast
of flame, of fire.

There is a clever creature
waiting in the folds of a book
a universe of thought
that break the back of mind
that snap a man's look
until he sees a vision clearly
of what is not there
and what cannot be
as he loses touch
with any kind of sensibility.

This clever creature
outwits bright minds
by bringing shrouds of clouds
across a man's brain
leading him to despair
guiding him onto the insane.

Clever minds
build a wall of books
to not be seen through
until there is no tomorrow
without a man's form
dangling from meat hooks.

There is the beast
of business, of activity
that occupies a man's space
by his doing
that takes away his time
that explains away his brain
with deception
until he becomes a brittle shell
with no heart
with only emptiness inside
a man as only his useless hide.
Many are the creatures
vile in their intent
determined to devour a man
to consume his body and soul
by the stroke of every hour.

How can a man
beat this army of beasts
their number immeasurable
their strength fierce, ruthless, terrible
as he walks through their jaws
their fangs dripping for his destruction.

Is there hope
for a man as he faces this treachery
or is he destined to be a wreck
a writhing ache in his eternity's debauchery.

As it is written,
"We can do all things through Christ Jesus
who strengthens us."

Economy of Being

In the economy of being
good consumes the evil
and evil buries the good
as the dawn of each day
ends in the darkness of dusk
as the darkness of each night
ends with the light of day.

So good is here and there
and evil is always somewhere
as the garden grows flowers alongside weeds
as each day brings death and life, life and death;
this too is the economy of being.

In the economy of being
you will always find
what you are looking for:
if you look for good
you fill find the good
and if you look for evil
you will find the evil.

It is either this
or that
one or the other
not both
and not anything else.

Do you want power or hope?

About the garden
the fragrance of a bush
brushes its lush perfume
across your mind
as beauty defines the wonder
of the moment
a beauty dripping wonder
into the moment.

So power
is a strength of appearance
the seen, the heard, the touched
the revealed by senses
as a throbbing rhythm
implodes time and space.

So hope
is a strength
in what can be found
in what is not apparent
not sensed by what you think you are
but gathered by the who that you are
as you explode with time and space
into a tingling elixir.

So, in the economy of being
there are the vapors
of what you think
escaping with the dawn
as the muscle of your might
tightens its grip
on shadows and shades of shadows
cast through the breathing breath
of what is there in the garden.

Of course, then
there is what is
and there is what is not
and both are alongside one another
as the day escapes into night
as night escapes into the light
of the garden, always the garden.

So, would you
rather be magical
or mysterious
one or the other
not both
either this or that?

As it is written, Jesus said,
"I am the true vine, and My Father
is the vine dresser. Every branch in Me
that does not bear fruit, He takes away
and every branch that bears fruit, He prunes it,
that it may bear more fruit."

Pure Beauty

By day
the mirror of the sky
through a crystal of blue
moves the heart
into wonder
but it is by night
in a deep indigo sky
that the soul sees
the forever
in being there.

It is a beauty
that the mind
cannot grasp.

It is
the tantalizing attraction
of this beauty
pure and encompassing
that arouses the vision
of the vastness
in what is the expanse.

How vast
this creature
called forever
alive in its purpose
powerful in its magnitude;
yet, its breath
is a delicate fragrance
an infusion of life-giving scent.

No passion
eclipses the radiant splendor
of forever.

When a flower blooms
the beauty of forever
excites a radiance
through the blossoming
an explosion of life
through the outstretched grandeur
reaching deep inside
an intimate space
where the rhythm
of being there
saturates a moment
given from the purely beauteous.

How lovely
the flowers
in the garden.

How much more wondrous
the blooms
of forevermore.

Dean C. Gardner

To be
in the presence
of beauty
grows the heart
with passion
as time tics
toward an end
of time and space
the moments
being momentary
while being in the presence
of True Beauty
the wonder
of face to face
with the Lord Almighty
without fear
grows the soul
toward an always jubilation
that endures
onto forevermore.

As it is written,
"In My Father's house
are many mansions.
I go to prepare a place for you there."

One Way, Only

There are ways
to the flight
of winged critters
as many ways
as they are.

Each way of flight
seems unique
to the kind and type
of winged critter.

Where the bumble bee
visits as it flies,
hovering over one spot
and then another
as if trying to decide
where to set down
the hornet
flies a short distance
sets down to walk around
and then flies another short distance
to set down
to walk around some more.

If a housefly
takes a liking
to someone's arm or leg
there is no escape
from its persistent flight
except its death.

The swallow darts
first in this direction
then in that
as if connecting the dots
to an invisible landscape.

When upon the water
the duck leaps
into the air
grabbing onto the sky
with a dire tenacity
while the goose
gallops across the water's surface
until it is airborne.

The woodpecker
downed in tuxedo black and white
with a brilliant red head
jettisons itself
from the side of a tree
climbing ever outward and upward
without dropping even a dot.

The flight
of the hawk
carves gyres in the sky
steady circles linked together
by the wind
its wings nearly motionless.

The common sparrow
has a frantic flight
from bush to sidewalk and sidewalk to bush
as it evades the human passers by
as it fetches crumbs
which are its mainstay.

There is the low flight
of the blackbird
across a wheat field
against the wind
as it labors
to gain distance
in an autumn sky.

So, there are
many different ways
the winged critters fly
each unique to its own kind.

But then,
as it is written,
Jesus said,
"I am the way, the truth and the life;
no one comes onto the Father except through me."

SUMMARY

1. The activity of man is either to uncover truth and choose his own meanings, or to adopt into the truth being chosen by its meaning.

2. To subvert the indwelling of truth as meaning, postures mind as the determinant of significance, which is being guilty of bad faith and self deception.

If a truth has no significance for the mind, that truth is dead.

Choice arises as the response to the synthesis of reality into the mind.

Choice initiates significance.

Consciousness and motive are inseparable.

Motive precedes and determines choice.

All responses to truths have consequences.

Consequence reshapes motive, alters choice, and is of the domain of truth.

The exercise of freedom is the process of choosing.

3. To adopt into the indwelling of truth as meaning, postures the substance behind and throughout the encompassing as the determinant of significance and results in self transcendence.

Truth and meaning are inseparable.

Meaning is a function of truth.

Truth is of the actual, is always transcendent, and is external to the mind. Through reason, the mind conceives reality – while through indwelling, self grasps meaning.

As truth indwells, self believes it, accepts it as it is, and adopts into it.

Truth does not become meaning through an appearance to the mind, but through the self adopting into it.

Through reason, the potential for self as reality is limited – while through the indwelling of truth, the potential for self as actuality is limitless.

The exercise of freedom is being an heir to truth.

Truth: the only hope for humankind.

As Jesus Christ said, "If you hold to my teaching, you are really my disciples. Then you will know the truth, and the truth will set you free."

CPSIA information can be obtained at www.ICGtesting.com
Printed in the USA
LVOW06s0528100414

381051LV00001B/50/P

9 781456 005733